Murder Mystery Short Stories

George Gentle

Published by George Gentle, 2024.

MURDER MYSTERY SHORT STORIES

First edition. June 30, 2024.

Copyright © 2024 George Gentle.

ISBN: 979-8227339768

Written by George Gentle.

Murder in the Seminary

Chapter 1:

Gregory Fitzsimmons, or Greg to his friends,sat alone at his desk, staring off into the distance as he listened to the sound of his classmates talking in hushed tones, their voices echoing off the stone walls of the seminary school. He had been raised by his mother in the small town they called home. His father had passed away when he was just a child, leaving his mother to raise him on her own.

As a result, Greg had grown up somewhat isolated from the other children in town. He had always been a quiet and introspective child, preferring the company of books over the noise and chaos of the outside world. It was this quiet nature that had led his mother to suggest that he attend the seminary school.

The seminary, with its strict code of conduct and focus on religious studies, had seemed like the perfect place for a young man like Greg. But as he sat there in his lonely silence, Greg couldn't help but wonder if he had made the right choice.

He turned his attention back to the class, trying to focus on the lecture being given by the stern-faced priest at the front of the room. But his mind kept wandering, drifting back to thoughts of his home and his mother. He missed her terribly, and often found himself longing for the simpler days of his childhood.

But even as he yearned for the comfort and security of home, Greg knew that he had a duty to fulfill. He had been raised to be a good and decent person, and he wanted to make a difference in the world. And so he resolved to work hard and do his best, even if it meant sacrificing his own happiness in the process.

As the class drew to a close, Greg stood up and gathered his things. He was determined to make the most of his time at the seminary, to become the kind of person his mother would be proud of. And with that thought in mind, he set off down the long, echoing hallway, ready to face whatever challenges lay ahead.

Chapter 2:

Greg was on his way to his theology class in the seminary when he heard a heated argument brewing. As he came closer, he could hear Father Augustas and one of the students, James, arguing about a young woman.

The young woman in question worked in the kitchen in the seminary and it appeared that there was some disagreement between Father Augustas and James about her conduct.

Greg paused, listening in as discreetly as possible, his curiosity piqued by the argument, but also his desire to help if he could. He waited until the argument ended before approaching James, who looked visibly upset.

"Is everything alright?" Greg asked kindly, trying to convey a sense of warmth and support.

James shook his head and began to explain the situation to Greg. Apparently, he had developed feelings for the young woman in question, but Father Augustas had warned him to keep his distance. The priest claimed that it would be inappropriate for James to pursue a relationship with her while he was studying in the seminary, and that it would be a "distraction."

James was clearly upset by Father Augustas' warning, and felt it was unfair that he couldn't even express his feelings for the young woman. Greg listened to James, and then offered some words of comfort.

"I understand why you're upset, James," he said. "But keep in mind that the seminary is a highly structured environment with strict rules. Perhaps Father Augustas has a point - it might be best to focus on your studies for now. You never know what the future holds."

James looked at Greg, and then nodded thoughtfully. "You're right," he said. "I'll try to put this aside and concentrate on my studies."

Greg smiled, feeling glad that he could help James. He then continued to his theology class.

Chapter 3:

That night Greg lay in his bed, staring up at the ceiling in the dimly lit room. His mind was racing and his body tense with anxiety. This was his first time away from home, and he was finding it difficult to adjust to the new surroundings. Everything was so unfamiliar - the sounds, the smells, the people.

He had tried to sleep, but it was impossible. He tossed and turned, feeling more and more frustrated. Finally, he couldn't take it anymore. He got up and decided to explore the seminary. He got dressed and quietly left his room.

As he walked down the hallway, he felt a sense of isolation and loneliness creeping in. He didn't know anyone here and he missed his mother terribly. He needed something to calm him down, and he remembered hearing that warm milk could help induce sleep.

He made his way to the kitchen, which was exactly where he remembered it to be. He felt a sense of relief wash over him as he made his way through the maze of corridors. The kitchen was dark, save for a small light above the stove. He was surprised to find that it was not locked, and he made his way in.

At first, he didn't see anyone, but then he noticed a figure sitting at the kitchen table. It was Father Joe, the seminary cook. Greg felt a jolt of fear at being caught, but Father Joe simply looked up and smiled.

"Can't sleep?" Father Joe asked kindly.

Greg nodded his head, feeling embarrassed.

"It's tough at first," Father Joe said. "But it gets better. Here, let me fix you a glass of warm milk."

Father Joe got up from his chair and went to the fridge. He poured a glass of milk and heated it on the stove. Greg watched as he added a pinch of cinnamon and a tablespoon of honey.

"When I can't sleep," Father Joe said, "I like to remember that God is watching over me. That always gives me peace of mind."

Greg listened as Father Joe spoke, feeling comforted by his words. He took the glass of warm milk and sipped it slowly, feeling the warmth spreading through his body. He suddenly felt very tired and realized that he was ready to sleep.

"Thanks, Father Joe," Greg said, feeling grateful. "I think I'll go back to bed now."

"Goodnight, Greg," Father Joe said with a smile. "Sleep well."

Greg made his way back to his room, feeling a sense of peace. He realized that he was not alone anymore and that he had a new family here at the seminary. He crawled back into bed, feeling relaxed and calm. He closed his eyes and drifted off to sleep, feeling grateful for the kind words and warm milk of Father Joe.

Chapter 4:

The following night Greg made his way to the kitchen again, unable to sleep he was hoping some more of Father Joe's warm milk would help. Father Joe was not there but what he saw made him want to scream, but no sound emanated from his throat.

As Greg stood frozen in the seminary school kitchen, his mind raced with a million thoughts. How did the body get there? Who could have done this? Was it an accident or a murder? He had heard about similar incidents in the past, but he never thought he would stumble upon one himself.

Greg tried to calm himself down and think rationally. He blocked the kitchen entrance with tables and chairs, so no one could come in and disturb the scene until the authorities arrived. He then called the police right away and explained the situation, giving the exact location and details of the scene.

He nervously waited for the police to arrive, praying that everything would be alright. As soon as they got there, they cordoned off the area, took pictures, and started collecting evidence. Greg was in shock and couldn't believe what was happening right in front of him.

The police asked Greg for his name and questioned him about how he found the body. He explained that he had come to the kitchen to get some warm milk to help him sleep when he saw the body on the kitchen floor and immediately called 999. They also asked him if he recognized the woman but he didn't, he had never seen her before.

The police finished up and declared it a murder investigation. They instructed Greg not to talk to nor tell anyone about the incident until further investigations have been carried out.

Greg left the kitchen still in shock, trying to process what just happened. He felt scared to imagine that a murderer was on the loose, and that he may be a potential target. Nevertheless, he was determined to be of any assistance the police may require during the investigation.

As he walked away from the kitchen, Greg could vividly picture the lifeless body of the young woman. Something inside him was telling him that the murder investigation was about to take a toll on his life in the Seminary.

Chapter 5:

Greg's heart thudded in his chest as he walked through the dark hallways of the seminary, following the sound of voices. The terrible news of the murdered woman in the kitchen had spread like wildfire through the seminary, leaving a sense of dread hanging over everyone. But now, as Greg made his way to the meeting with a detective, his senses were sharpened, and he could feel his pulse racing.

As he turned the corner, he saw a man sitting at a table, poring over what looked like files. The man was slightly older, with a thinning gray hairline and a craggy, careworn face. Despite the man's age, there was something about him that exuded a sense of command and authority.

"Hello, I'm Greg," Greg said, extending his hand as he drew near the table.

The man looked up, appraising Greg with a steady gaze. "Alwyn Jones, Detective," he said, shaking Greg's hand. "Please, have a seat."

As Greg took a seat across from the Detective, he felt a sense of unease wash over him. He wasn't used to dealing with detectives, and the fact that he was now talking to one in the wake of a terrible crime put him on edge.

"I understand that you were in the seminary at the time of the murder?" Alwyn asked, flipping open a notebook.

"Yes," Greg said, feeling his pulse quicken. "I had gone to the kitchen to get a glass of warm milk to help me sleep when I saw the body."

"Did you see anyone else in the area at the time of the murder?"

"No, I didn't. I was the only one there."

Alwyn nodded, jotting something down in his notebook. "Can you describe the body?"

Greg paused, a lump forming in his throat. It was difficult enough coming to terms with what he had seen, let alone having to describe it to a detective. "It was a woman, she... she was lying on the floor in a pool of blood."

Alwyn's expression hardened. "Did you touch anything in the kitchen?"

"No. I didn't want to disturb anything."

"Good," Alwyn said, closing his notebook. "It's important that we preserve any evidence that we find."

Greg watched as Alwyn rose to his feet, drawing his coat around him. "We'll be in touch if we need to ask you anything further," the detective said, placing a hand on Greg's shoulder. "In the meantime, stay out of trouble."

As Alwyn walked away, Greg slumped back in his seat, feeling a sense of desolation washing over him. It was clear that the detective was a man of steely intellect, and Greg knew that the investigation would be in good hands. But as he took the long walk back to his room, he couldn't shake the sense of unease that lingered within him. The memory of the body, and the events of the day, would haunt him for a long time to come.

Chapter 6:

Father Augustus stood silent in front of the lifeless form of the woman stretched out on a gurney, observing her features with a look of sorrow and resignation etched onto his face. The hair was matted with blood, the pallor of the skin hinting at the tragedy that had befallen her.

After examining the body carefully, he spoke in a hushed tone to Alwyn Jones standing next to him. "Her name was Elizabeth," he said, his voice heavy with grief. "She was one of our kitchen workers, a wonderful young woman."

Alwyn nodded, his expression unreadable as he scribbled something down in his notepad.

"Father, do you know if she had any enemies or was there anyone who would want to hurt her?" he asked, looking up from his notes.

Father Augustus didn't miss a beat. "No, she was well-liked by everyone. But there was one young seminarian who had some... strong feelings for her."

The detective looked up at him, interested. "Who was that?'

"James," replied the Father. "He was visibly upset when he found out about her passing. He's a good boy, but he can be somewhat impulsive at times."

Alwyn Jones absorbed the information thoughtfully, before thanking Father Augustus and walking away. As he watched the detective leave, Father Agustus couldn't help but feel a sense of foreboding settling over him. Elizabeth's death was a tragedy, one that would rock the seminary to its core. But if there was someone among them who had a hand in it, then whoever it was needed to be apprehended, and quickly.

He walked back to his office, trying to collect his thoughts. As he sat down at his desk, he reached for his rosary and began to pray. The image of James, the young seminarian, came to his mind - someone he had taken under his wing and tried to nurture in the faith.

But now, as the investigation into Elizabeth's death continued, Father Augustus couldn't help but have doubts. He hoped that James's feelings for Elizabeth had been purely innocent, but deep down inside him, he knew that sometimes love could take a deadly turn.

Chapter 7:

James sat nervously in Father Augustus' office, his palms sweaty with anxiety. Across from him sat the kindly priest and the detective, Alwyn Jones.The news of Elizabeth's death had shaken him to his core, and the fact that he had been a suspect in her murder only added to his distress. He knew he needed to set the record straight and provide an alibi for the time of the murder.

"James, can you tell me where you were at the time of Elizabeth's death?" Alwyn Jones asked, his gentle voice softening James' nerves.

"I was at the Golden Goose pub with my friends Robert and David," James replied, his voice shaking. "We left the seminary around 7 pm and didn't come back until curfew at 11 pm."

Alwyn nodded. "And can anyone vouch for your whereabouts during that time?"

"Yes, Peggy, the barmaid at the Golden Goose," James replied. "She served us drinks and we were there until 10:30 pm."

Father Agustus listened intently, taking note of the details as James spoke. He had known James for a while and found him to be a good-hearted and open boy. The fact that he had an alibi made him feel relieved.

The coroner had placed Elizabeth's death at 09:30pm the same time James was at the pub. The pub's barmaid, Peggy Althrope, gave a statement saying that James, Robert, and David had been at the Golden Goose for several hours until around 10:30 PM, which checked out with James's recollection.

Alwyn knew that James was not a suspect anymore, thanks to his alibi. It was a massive relief for James and a massive disappointment for the detective, who was hoping to find the murderer amongst the seminary students.

Later that night Father Augustus sat down to write a letter to James. He wanted to offer his condolences and support after the tragic loss of Elizabeth. He also added in the letter that James had exhibited bravery by stepping forward and providing an alibi. It showed that the boy was honorable and courageous.

As Father Agustus finished the note, a sense of peace settled over him. The investigation into Elizabeth's death was continuing, but James was no longer a suspect, and the truth would soon be revealed.

Chapter 8:

Greg had heard rumors of Robert's infatuation with James, but it was only after he dug deeper that he found firm evidence to back it up. He had uncovered a stash of love letters in Robert room, that Robert had written to James but never sent, desperately pouring his heart out to his friend.

The revelation was a shock to Greg, but he knew he needed to tread carefully. After all, the case was still in progress, and he could not afford to jump to conclusions.

Greg couldn't shake the feeling that Robert was the killer. Every piece of evidence seemed to point in his direction, and Greg knew that he needed to share his suspicions with Detective Alwyn Jones.

Alwyn was already well-versed in the case and had been following the investigation closely. When Greg laid out his findings and evidence on Robert, Alwyn listened intently, making notes in his notepad.

"Interesting," Alwyn murmured. "But it is only circumstantial evidence, there is no real proof of his guilt"

Greg nodded. "I understand that, sir. But I truly believe that Robert is guilty and that he acted out of jealousy towards Elizabeth."

Alwyn raised an eyebrow. "Jealousy? Towards Elizabeth? And what about James?"

"Robert was infatuated with James," Greg explained. " I found love letters that Robert had written to him. James was never interested, but Robert became obsessed. It's possible that he saw Elizabeth as a threat.

As Greg left the meeting with Alwyn, he felt a sense of hope wash over him. He knew that they still had a long way to go to build a solid case against Robert, but at least now he had a target to concentrate on.

Chapter 9:

The next evening Greg and Detective Alwyn Jones sat down together. They knew that they had to catch Robert in the act of confessing to the murder of Elizabeth. Alwyn suggested that they let it be known that Greg had a letter from Elizabeth , the letter would claim that Elizabeth had found out about Robert's feelings towards James and that she was going to tell Father Augustus. When Robert tried to find the letter, Greg could confront him and try and get him to confess.

Greg was hesitant at first, but he realized that they had to go the extra mile to solve this case. They decided to go ahead with the plan and began to put things in motion.

The next day, as Greg returned from prayers he heard some noises coming from his room and found that the door was slightly open .With a hint of suspicion, Greg slowly approached the door and looked through the narrow opening. His eyes widened as he saw Robert rummaging through his belongings.

Without missing a beat, Greg pushed the door fully open and confronted Robert "What are you doing in my room, Robert ?"

Startled by Greg's sudden appearance, Robert stood up and straightened his clothes, "I was just looking for a letter, Greg. It's from Elizabeth."

Greg's expression turned to one of confusion. "What letter?" he asked, puzzled. "I don't have any letter," he added, observing Robert's uncertain body language.

Robert hesitated for a moment before replying, "It's nothing, really. I overheard Detective Alwyn Jones mentioned to Father Augustus that you had found an unopened letter written by Elizabeth"

Greg narrowed his eyes and asked, "Why would you be searching for a letter Robert ? And why do you even care about Elizabeth's letters?"

Robert fidgeted and seemed hesitant to answer. Finally, he opened his mouth and said, "I just wanted to check if the letter contained something important.

"I don't think I believe you, I think you're hiding something from me. Something to do with her murder" said Greg.

Robert looked pale and visibly shaken. After a few minutes, he began to speak out loud.

"I can't believe she found out," he muttered. "I had to do it. I couldn't let her ruin everything for me, but it was an accident I swear".

Chapter 10:

Greg listened as Robert confessed to the murder of Elizabeth. How he had been struggling with his feelings for James for several weeks, trying his best to keep them hidden from his friends and classmates in the seminary. However, somehow Elizabeth had found out and began to taunt him about his sexuality, he found it increasingly difficult to keep his emotions in check.

One night, after spending some time with his friends in the Golden Goose public house, he had slipped away to confront Elizabeth in the seminary kitchen. He was hoping to talk things out with her and get her to stop tormenting him about his feelings for James.

As soon as he arrived in the kitchen, Elizabeth started to provoke him, hurling insults and taunts at him. Robert tried his best to remain calm and composed, but her words cut him like a knife. He felt his anger and frustration building inside of him.

In that moment Robert's anger boiled over, and he picked up the kettle , which had been boiling on the kitchen stove,and hit Elizabeth in a fit of rage. He knew that as she fell to the floor, he had killed her, panicked and ran out of the kitchen.

When Greg heard Robert's confession he was initially shocked and saddened, after hearing Robert out, Greg suggested that they go see Father Augustus, the senior priest at the seminary, to hear Robert's confession and ask for advice. Father Augustus was known for his compassionate and non-judgmental approach, and Greg thought that he would be the best person to turn to in this situation.

Chapter 11:

When they arrived at Father Augustus' office, Greg explained the situation to him and asked if he could hear Robert's confession. Father Augustus agreed, and he listened attentively as Robert opened up about his struggles with his sexuality,his feelings for James and the murder of Elizabeth.

Father Augustus responded with empathy and compassion, reminding Robert that God loved him no matter what and the right thing to do was to accept his guilt and go to the police and confess his crime.

The trio headed to the police station and met with Detective Alwyn Jones. They explained the situation to him and Robert confessed to his crime. At first,Alwyn Jones was shocked to hear Robert's admission, but he was glad that Robert had decided to come forth and accept responsibility for his actions.

As Robert spoke, he felt a heavy weight being lifted off his shoulders. He knew that he had done the right thing, even if it was difficult.

Father Augustus gave Robert his blessings and assured him that forgiveness is available to everyone, including him. With tears in his eyes, Robert felt a sense of redemption as he accepted the consequences of his actions.

In the end, Robert was grateful for the support of Greg and Father Augustus. He knew that he couldn't have gone through the ordeal alone, and their presence gave him the strength to move forward and accept the consequences of his actions. Robert knew that it wouldn't be easy, but he was determined to become a better person and hoped that one day, he would find a way to make things right.

THE END.

Body in the woods. A Brother Thomas Mystery.

Chapter 1: The Mystery of the Young Girl

Brother Thomas, a devoted Benedictine monk of St. Cuthbert's Monastery, was known for his love for nature. He often spent his days wandering through the nearby woods, collecting herbs and plants for the monastery's apothecary.

One crisp autumn morning, as Brother Thomas made his way through the dense forest, he stumbled upon a sight that would forever change his peaceful existence. There, lying among the flowers and fallen leaves, was the lifeless body of a young man. Shocked and saddened by the discovery, Brother Thomas knelt beside the body to offer up a prayer. As the sun began to set and the shadows lengthened around him, Brother Thomas carried the body back to St. Cuthbert's Monastery, he sent word to the town's sheriff and began to prepare the body for a Christian burial.

As he gently removed the tattered clothing from the young man's form, he was struck by a sudden realisation - beneath the boy's garments lay the delicate features of a young girl. Confusion and disbelief washed over Brother Thomas as he struggled to comprehend the mystery before him.

Who was this young girl, dressed as a boy and lying alone in the depths of the forest? What tragic circumstances had led her to this lonely fate? Questions swirled in Brother Thomas's mind as he carefully washed and dressed the girl's body, his hands trembling with a mixture of sorrow and curiosity.

Word of the mysterious discovery spread quickly through the monastery, and soon the abbot summoned Brother Thomas to his chambers to hear the full account of what had transpired in the woods. Seated before the abbot, Brother Thomas recounted the details of his fateful encounter, his voice steady despite the turmoil within him. The abbot listened intently, his wise eyes searching Brother Thomas's face for any hint of deceit or doubt.

After a long moment of silence, the abbot spoke, his voice grave yet compassionate. "Brother Thomas, this is a most troubling discovery indeed. We must unravel the mystery of this young girl's fate and bring justice to her memory. You have shown great courage in bringing this matter to light, and for that, I commend you."

Determined to uncover the truth behind the girl's untimely death, Brother Thomas embarked on a journey of investigation and discovery. Little did he know that his quest for justice would test not only his faith and resolve but that it would lead him deep into the heart of darkness lurking within men's souls.

Chapter 2: Whispers in the Woods

The monastery was a place of deep contemplation and rarely a host to the unexpected, but the discovery of the young girl had cast a shadow of mystery over its stone walls. The monks, who had committed themselves to a life of routine and prayer, found themselves whispering about the girl's identity and the secrets she might have held.

Brother Thomas, however, found no solace in speculation. The girl's delicate features, framed by a tangle of chestnut hair, seemed to haunt his every thought. He knew that the answers he sought would not be found within the monastery's walls, but out there, in the woods that had kept her secret until now.

The following day, Brother Thomas rose before dawn and ventured back into the forest. The air was thick with mist, and the trees stood like silent sentinels guarding their domain. As he retraced his steps from the previous day, he couldn't shake the feeling that he was not alone; that the forest itself was watching him, aware of his quest for truth.

He reached the spot where he had found the girl and paused, looking around for any signs of her life before death. It was then that he noticed the remnants of a makeshift camp hidden beneath a canopy of oak leaves—a small, extinguished fire pit surrounded by a few scattered belongings.

Among the items, Brother Thomas found a worn leather journal. The pages, though dampened by the forest's embrace, held the secret of the girl's masquerade. Her name was Elanor, and she had been running from a destiny that had been forced upon her—a marriage to a cruel lord whom she had never met. Disguised as a boy, she had fled her home in the dead of night, seeking refuge in the anonymity of the woods.

As Brother Thomas read Elanor's final entries, a picture of her life began to emerge. She spoke of the freedom she found in her solitude, but also of the fear that pursued her like a relentless shadow. Her words were filled with a longing for peace and an end to her flight.

But how had her journey led to her untimely death? There were no clues to suggest violence; no wounds or signs of struggle. Brother Thomas pondered the possibility of illness or an accident, but something in his heart told him there was more to her story—a piece of the puzzle that was still missing.

Determined to lay Elanor's memory to rest with the dignity she deserved, Brother Thomas made a vow before the silent woods. He would find the truth of Elanor's past and the cause of her death. As he closed the journal and wrapped it in his robe, the wind seemed to carry a soft whisper through the trees, as if the forest itself was urging him on. With a heavy heart, Brother Thomas returned to the monastery, the journal his silent companion. He knew the task ahead would not be easy, for the world outside the monastery was one of complexity and danger. But for Elanor, and the peace of her soul, he was prepared to face whatever lay beyond the safety of St. Cuthbert's stone walls.

Chapter 3: Beyond the Monastery Gates

The morning sun had barely touched the stained-glass windows of the chapel when Brother Thomas approached Abbot Michael to seek his blessing. The monastery, usually a beacon of tranquility, was abuzz with the news of the young girl's mysterious death, and the Abbot was not immune to the unsettling atmosphere.

"Father," Brother Thomas began, his voice a mere whisper against the choral hymns echoing from the chapel, "I request leave to journey beyond our walls, to seek the truth about Elanor."

The Abbot regarded him with a measured gaze. "Brother Thomas, your heart is troubled. This is not our way," he replied with a gentle firmness.

"But Father, her soul may not find peace until her story is told. It is not only for her, but for the sanctity of our faith, that we must act," Brother Thomas implored, the journal pressed against his chest as if it were a holy relic.

Abbot Michael's eyes softened, understanding the weight of the task Brother Thomas felt called to undertake. After a moment of silent prayer, he finally nodded. "Go with God, Brother Thomas. Seek out the answers you need, but remember the path of righteousness in all you do."

With the Abbot's blessing, Brother Thomas prepared for his journey. He donned a simple traveler's cloak over his monastic habit and filled a satchel with provisions—bread, cheese, and a small flask of water. The other monks watched in silent reverence as Brother Thomas stepped towards the heavy oak doors of the monastery, the boundary between his world of devotion and the vast, unknown lands beyond.

The forest greeted him like an old friend, the path familiar yet foreboding with the weight of his mission. Brother Thomas followed the whispering trails, the journal his guide, leading him towards the village that Elanor had called home.

It was a day's walk to the village, and as the monastery spire disappeared behind him, Brother Thomas felt a pang of solitude unlike any he had known within his cloistered life. The world outside was vibrant and chaotic, filled with the sounds of life and the bustling of humanity.

Upon reaching the village, Brother Thomas was struck by the sharp gaze of the villagers. Their eyes were wary, their whispers curious and tinged with suspicion. A stranger, especially a monk, was an uncommon sight in this secluded part of the country.

He made his way to the local inn, a modest establishment of timber and thatch, hoping to glean some information about Elanor's family or her betrothed lord. The innkeeper, a rotund man with a ruddy complexion, was initially reticent but thawed under Brother Thomas's gentle demeanor.

"Aye, I knew of Elanor," the innkeeper said, his voice low. "A spirited lass. 'Twas a dark day when word came she'd vanished. And her father, the old baron, well, he's not been the same since."

The innkeeper's eyes darted around the room before he leaned in closer. "They say it was the lord she was to marry who brought the darkness upon her. A cruel man, Lord Edmund. His lands lie to the north, and his heart, some say, is as cold as the stones of his keep."

Armed with this new knowledge, Brother Thomas knew where he must head next. He thanked the innkeeper and stepped out of the warm glow of the inn into the cooling dusk. His journey had only just begun, and the path ahead promised to be fraught with more peril than the silent woods he had left behind.

With a prayer on his lips for strength and protection, Brother Thomas set his sights on the north, towards the foreboding lands of Lord Edmund, where he hoped to uncover the final chapters of Elanor's tragic tale.

Chapter 4: The Shadow of Lord Edmund's Keep

The road to Lord Edmund's lands was a lonely one, a narrow ribbon winding through a countryside that grew increasingly bleak with each passing mile. The laughter and warmth of the inn seemed a world away as Brother Thomas ventured into a region where the very air seemed tinged with unease. Villages were few and far between, and the peasants he passed worked the fields with heads bowed, their eyes reflecting a wariness that spoke of hard lives and the fear of their lord.

Brother Thomas spent his nights under the stars, sheltered by the canopy of trees or the eaves of abandoned cottages. He used the solitude to reflect on the scriptures and the mystery that lay before him, finding comfort in his faith. Elanor's journal, a constant companion, was read and reread by the light of his small campfire, each word committed to memory, each sentence a clue to the girl's fate.

On the third day, the imposing silhouette of Lord Edmund's keep appeared on the horizon, its towers like jagged teeth against the grey sky. A shiver ran down Brother Thomas's spine—not from the chill in the air, but from the realisation that he was drawing closer to the heart of the mystery.

He reached the outskirts of the keep by midday, where the heavy scent of iron and smoke hung in the air. The massive structure was surrounded by a high stone wall, and the main gate was guarded by men-at-arms whose suspicious glares were as unwelcoming as the spiked portcullis above them.

Brother Thomas approached with caution, offering a humble nod to the guards. "Peace be with you. I seek an audience with Lord Edmund," he said, his voice steady despite the flutter of apprehension in his chest. One of the guards snorted in derision, but the other, perhaps out of respect for Brother Thomas's holy orders, grunted and disappeared inside the gatehouse. Moments later, the gate creaked open just enough to allow the monk entrance.

Inside the walls, the keep was austere and unadorned, the courtyard empty save for a few servants scurrying about their tasks. Brother Thomas was led to a small antechamber to await the lord, the air heavy with the scent of damp stone and burning torches.

Finally, the door swung open, and Lord Edmund entered. He was a tall man, broad-shouldered with a presence that filled the room. His eyes, cold and calculating, appraised Brother Thomas with open suspicion.

"What business does a monk have with me?" Lord Edmund's voice was as sharp as the blade at his side.

Brother Thomas met the lord's gaze with a calm he did not feel. "My lord, I come seeking answers about a young girl named Elanor, who was once betrothed to you. I found her body in the woods near St. Cuthbert's Monastery, and I wish to understand the circumstances of her death."

A flicker of something crossed Lord Edmund's face—surprise, perhaps, or annoyance—but it was gone as quickly as it had appeared.

"Elanor is dead?" he said, his voice betraying no emotion. "You're certain of this?"

"I am, my lord. And as God is my witness, I will see her laid to rest with the truth known," Brother Thomas replied, his resolve steeling him against the oppressive air of the keep.

Lord Edmund considered him for a long moment before nodding to the guard. "Bring him to the library. We will discuss this matter further."

The library was a stark room lined with shelves of books and scrolls. As the door closed behind them, leaving them in seclusion, Lord Edmund turned to Brother Thomas.

"Speak then, monk. Tell me everything you know," he commanded, his voice echoing slightly off the stone walls.

Chapter 5: Revelations in the Keep

The library of Lord Edmund's keep, with its high, arched windows and the flickering dance of torchlight upon row upon row of ancient tomes, felt like a world apart from the rest of the austere fortress. Here, in this sanctuary of knowledge, Brother Thomas began to unravel the tale of Elanor's fate.

"My lord," Brother Thomas started, his voice echoing slightly in the hallowed space, "I found Elanor's body in a clearing, not far from St. Cuthbert's Monastery. The woodland flowers were woven into her hair, as if she had been laid to rest with care, not discarded like refuse. There was no sign of violence upon her person, but rather it appeared she had succumbed to some unseen malady or profound sorrow."

Lord Edmund's face remained impassive, but his eyes narrowed slightly, a sign that the news had struck some chord within him. "And what makes you believe her story is mine to know?" he asked, the edge in his voice sharp as a knife.

"Elanor was to be your bride, my lord," Brother Thomas replied, meeting the lord's steely gaze. "The bond between betrothed is sacred, and I believed you would want to know of her passing. Moreover, the circumstances of her death are most mysterious, and any light you could shed upon her life would aid in understanding how she met her end."

For a long moment, Lord Edmund said nothing, his face a mask that concealed the tumult surely raging within. Then, with a heavy sigh, he walked to the great window that looked out over his lands, his back to Brother Thomas.

"I knew Elanor well," he began, his voice softer now, tinged with an emotion Brother Thomas could not quite place. "I watched her grow from a child into a woman of grace and beauty. I had hoped to make her my wife, to bring her nobility and strength to my side. But Elanor's heart was her own, and she did not love me."

Brother Thomas listened intently, aware that the lord was revealing more than he likely intended.

"She loved another—a blacksmith named Mathew," Lord Edmund continued, his hands clasped behind his back. "He was a commoner, but what he lacked in title, he made up for with a kind of earnest passion that seemed to captivate her completely."

"And this Mathew," Brother Thomas prompted gently, "where is he now?"

Lord Edmund turned from the window, his expression dark. "He disappeared. Around the same time Elanor did. Everyone thought they had run off together, that they had chosen love over duty and station. But if you found her alone..." His voice trailed off, and for the first time, Brother Thomas saw the façade crack, a glimpse of the pain lurking beneath.

"My lord, if I may be so bold," Brother Thomas said, stepping forward, "perhaps Mathew's disappearance is linked to Elanor's death. If we could find him, we might uncover the truth of what happened."

Lord Edmund regarded Brother Thomas with a newfound respect. "Yes, perhaps you are right, Brother. If you are willing to continue this search, I will grant you any assistance you require. It is the least I can do for Elanor's memory."

Brother Thomas bowed his head. "I am resolved to see this quest through, my lord. With your leave, I will seek out Mathew the blacksmith and bring clarity to these dark waters."

"Then you have my blessing, Brother Thomas," Lord Edmund declared, a solemn note in his voice. "Find the truth, for Elanor, for her family, and for all those who loved her."

With that, Brother Thomas was dismissed, stepping out of the keep with a new purpose.

Chapter 6: The Blacksmith's Tale

Brother Thomas's journey to Saint Jude's infirmary was one shrouded in contemplation. The image of Elanor, a maiden felled by unseen forces, haunted his every step, and the weight of Lord Edmund's sorrowful confession pressed heavily upon his heart.

Upon arriving at the infirmary, a humble building of whitewashed walls and thatched roof, Brother Thomas was greeted by the scent of herbs and the quiet murmurs of the ailing. Sister Bernadette, the matron of the infirmary, led him through the rows of beds to where Mathew lay, his once-strong body rendered frail by injury.

Mathew, with bandages wrapped around his head, looked up with a mixture of confusion and wariness as Brother Thomas approached. The monk offered a gentle smile and sat beside the bed, his hands folded in his lap.

"Mathew the blacksmith, I presume?" Brother Thomas began, his voice soft. "I am Brother Thomas, and I come seeking answers about Elanor, whom you loved."

Mathew's eyes, clouded with pain, sharpened at the mention of Elanor's name. "Elanor," he breathed, a tremor in his voice. "Is she safe? Have you news of her?"

Brother Thomas's heart ached with the duty he bore. "I am deeply sorry, Mathew. I found her in the woods near Saint Cuthbert's. She had passed from this world."

The colour drained from Mathew's face, and a look of profound grief washed over him. "No," he whispered, tears brimming in his eyes. "We were to meet that day, in the woods. She was late... I waited for her, but she never came. Then someone struck me from behind. I remember nothing more until I awoke injured, and made my way here."

Brother Thomas reached out, placing a comforting hand on Mathew's. "Who would do this to you? Do you remember aught of your assailant?"

Mathew shook his head, his expression tormented. "I saw no one. I heard nothing. It's as if the blow came from the shadows themselves."

The monk's brow furrowed in thought. "Elanor was disguised as a boy when I found her," he revealed, watching Mathew closely.

A flash of understanding crossed Mathew's face. "Aye, that was our plan," he confirmed, his voice a hoarse whisper. "To avoid drawing eyes to our meeting. She was to dress as a lad and slip away unnoticed. But if she never arrived..."

Brother Thomas considered the implications of this new information. "Someone must have known of your plans, someone who wished to prevent your union."

Mathew's hands clenched into fists, the knuckles white. "But who? And why?"

"That, I cannot yet say," Brother Thomas admitted. "But I vow to you, on my faith and my order, I will seek out the truth. Elanor's spirit shall not rest uneasy, nor shall those who loved her live in the shadow of this mystery."

Mathew nodded, his eyes reflecting a deep sorrow mingled with gratitude. "Thank you, Brother Thomas. Elanor was everything to me. I would have given all to protect her."

Rising from his seat, Brother Thomas offered a final, reassuring nod to the blacksmith. "Rest and heal, Mathew. Your part in this tale is not yet done."

With the blacksmith's story etched into his mind, Brother Thomas stepped out of the infirmary into the waning light of day, his resolve steeled. The pieces of the puzzle were slowly coming together, but with each revelation, the web of intrigue seemed to grow more complex.

Chapter 7: A Baron's Grief

The village that lay in the shadow of the baron's modest manor was quiet as Brother Thomas made his way through its narrow streets. The news of Elanor's death hung heavy in the air, a pall of sorrow that touched every villager he passed. The baron, once a man of influence and wealth, now faced not only the decline of his fortunes but the crushing blow of his daughter's untimely demise.

As Brother Thomas approached the manor, the somber tolling of the chapel bell echoed through the crisp air, a mournful dirge that seemed to resonate with the very beat of the earth. The manor itself, though still grand, bore the subtle signs of decay—vines creeping up its stone walls, shingles missing from its roof.

The monk was admitted entry by a servant whose eyes were red-rimmed from weeping. The household was draped in fabrics of black and grey, the traditional colours of mourning, and the air was thick with the scent of incense intended to guide Elanor's soul to the heavens.

Baron Geoffrey and his wife, Lady Isobel, were seated in the great hall, a vast room that seemed to swallow the light, its hearth cold and empty. They rose as Brother Thomas entered, their faces lined with grief that no words could ease.

"Brother Thomas," the baron began, his voice but a whisper of the commanding tone it once carried, "you bring news of our daughter. We have heard she is gone from this world. Tell us, how did she die?"

Brother Thomas bowed his head, his heart heavy. "My lord, my lady, it grieves me to confirm that your daughter has indeed passed. I found her in the woods, laid to rest amidst the flowers. There were no marks upon her, no sign of struggle. It is a mystery I am resolved to unravel."

Lady Isobel's hand flew to her mouth, stifling a sob, as her husband's face grew taut with a mix of sorrow and anger. "Elanor was our hope," the baron said, his voice growing stronger with the swell of his emotions. "She was to marry Lord Edmund, to secure our family's future. Now... now all is lost."

Brother Thomas noted the baron's emphasis on the marriage's importance, not just as a union of love, but as a lifeline for their dwindling fortunes. "My lord," he said gently, "I understand that the match with Lord Edmund was vital to your estate. But did Elanor share your enthusiasm for this alliance?"

The baron exchanged a pained look with his wife before turning back to Brother Thomas, his eyes dark with remembered conversations. "Elanor was... reluctant," he admitted. "She was headstrong, full of dreams of love and passion. She spoke often of Mathew, the blacksmith."

"And what of Mathew?" Brother Thomas asked. "He lies injured in Saint Jude's infirmary, attacked on the same day Elanor was to meet him."

The baron's brow furrowed. "Attacked, you say? That is ill news indeed. Mathew is a good man, though not the match we desired for our daughter."

Lady Isobel, who had remained silent, her grief a silent shroud, finally spoke. "Elanor would not heed our counsel," she said, her voice laced with the sharp sting of loss. "She believed her heart knew better than our wisdom. Oh, my child, what has befallen you?"

Brother Thomas stood, his resolve as firm as the stone walls that surrounded them. "I will find out who is responsible for Elanor's death and Mathew's attack. Someone sought to sever their bond, and in doing so, has brought great suffering to all."

Chapter 8: Whispers and Shadows

The great hall, once a place of feasts and laughter, now seemed to Brother Thomas a tomb, echoing with the silent screams of a family's shattered dreams. He murmured a prayer for the souls of the departed and for the strength to unravel the tangled skein of fate that had led to Elanor's death.

After taking his leave from the grieving baron and his wife, Brother Thomas stepped out into the twilight, where the last fingers of sunlight grasped futilely at the encroaching night. The village, though quiet, was not asleep; rather, it seemed to hold its breath, awaiting the next twist in its tale of woe.

Brother Thomas made his way to the local tavern, a place where whispers flowed as freely as ale, and where, if fortune favored him, he might glean some insight into the mystery at hand. The tavern, The Crooked Ploughman, was a low-beamed establishment that hummed with the subdued conversations of its patrons.

He found a seat in a shadowed corner, a hooded figure amidst the common folk. Here, the villagers spoke more freely, unaware of the monk in their midst. Brother Thomas listened, his ears attuned to the fragments of speech that drifted to him over the din of clinking cups and the crackle of the hearth fire.

"...never saw her much with that Edmund," one weathered farmer said, scratching at his beard. "Always thought she had eyes for the smithy."

"Aye, but the baron had plans, big plans," another villager chimed in, his voice tinged with a mixture of pity and scorn. "Wanted to marry her off to that lord, secure his lands again."

"And what of the smith?" a third voice asked, hushed and conspiratorial. "Heard he took a nasty blow to the head, didn't see it coming."

Brother Thomas sipped at the small ale he had purchased, his mind racing. The villagers' words confirmed what he had suspected: Elanor's heart belonged to Mathew, not Lord Edmund, and the baron's ambitions had been well-known.

He was about to depart when a new thread of conversation caught his attention, a whisper as delicate and dangerous as a spider's web.

"...they say the woods are haunted," a woman's voice trembled, barely audible above the tavern's hum. "That Saint Cuthbert's woods hold spirits that meddle in the affairs of men."

A chill ran down Brother Thomas's spine. Superstition was common among the folk, but in times of darkness, such beliefs could point to truths otherwise overlooked.

He decided he would visit the woods come morning, to walk the paths Elanor had trodden and to seek out any sign of the supernatural that the villagers so feared.

Brother Thomas, weary from his long journey, and with his hood drawn low to shield his identity, approached the innkeeper with a humble smile. "Good sir," he began, his voice gentle and warm, "I seek shelter for the night, if you would be so kind. My journey has been long, and the road ahead is dark. A simple room, a place to rest my weary bones, is all I ask for." The innkeeper, a stout man with a warm smile replied, "Of course, We have a cosy room available for you, with a soft bed and a warm hearth to chase away the chill of the night. May it bring you peace and comfort on your travels". As Brother Thomas settled into his humble quarters, the crackling fire in the hearth cast a warm glow over the room, and the scent of freshly baked bread wafted in from the kitchen. Grateful for the comfort and hospitality of the inn, Brother Thomas said a prayer of thanks. As he lay in his soft bed that night, Brother Thomas pondered the day's revelations. The baron's financial desperation, the thwarted love of Elanor and Mathew, the whispered fears of the villagers—all were pieces of a puzzle that, when complete, would reveal the hand that had so cruelly snatched Elanor from this world.

Sleep, however, proved elusive, for the monk's mind was ablaze with questions and possibilities, each more troubling than the last. In the quiet of his room, with only the Almighty as his witness, Brother Thomas vowed to bring the darkness to light, to avenge a maiden's death and to restore peace to a land gripped by fear and sorrow.

Chapter 9: The Path Through Saint Cuthbert's Woods

The dawn greeted Brother Thomas with a sky washed in hues of pink and orange, painting a serene backdrop to the day's grim task. After partaking in morning prayers, he set out, equipped only with his faith and the determination to uncover the truth behind Elanor's untimely demise.

Saint Cuthbert's Woods loomed at the edge of the village, a dense thicket of ancient trees and tangled underbrush that had stood watch over the land for centuries. Legend held that Saint Cuthbert himself had once blessed these woods, and in the daylight, it was easy to imagine the woods as a place of sanctuary.

But Brother Thomas was not swayed by the deceptive calm of the morning light. He knew that beneath the beauty of the woods, darker forces could be at work, and secrets lay hidden in the quiet glades and shadowy nooks.

As he entered the woods, the monk took a moment to offer a silent prayer to the Almighty for guidance and protection. Then, with a measured step, he began to walk the path he believed Elanor had taken on her last day among the living.

The path was well-trodden, a testament to the villagers' frequent travels through the woods for foraging and hunting. Brother Thomas examined the ground meticulously, searching for any disturbance in the earth or foliage that might suggest a struggle or flight.

He moved with purpose, his eyes scanning the ground, the trees, the very air around him for any sign out of the ordinary. Fallen branches and leaves, the scuttle of woodland creatures, the distant call of a bird—all were noted and considered.

As he reached a clearing where wildflowers grew in abundance, Brother Thomas paused. This, was the place where he had found Elanor's body, a natural bower fit for a maiden of her gentleness and beauty. He knelt, inspecting the area with a practiced eye. The flowers themselves showed no sign of being crushed or disturbed, as one might expect had there been a struggle here.

He then noticed something peculiar—a single flower, unlike the others, with petals as black as a raven's wing, standing in stark contrast to the vibrant colours around it. It was a Nightshade, a beautiful yet toxic bloom. Brother Thomas knew the plant well; it was not native to this area, and its presence here was an anomaly.

With careful hands, Brother Thomas collected the Nightshade, wrapping its stem in a piece of cloth. This could very well be a clue, possibly the means by which Elanor met her end, given the plant's poisonous properties.

His search continued, and as he ventured further, he discovered a small brook where the water flowed over pebbles and stones, whispering secrets only the forest could understand. There, caught on a jagged rock, was a scrap of fabric, torn and frayed.

Brother Thomas examined the fabric, noting its quality and the pattern of its weave. It was a course cloth, the kind Elanor was wearing the day he found her. He carefully preserved the fabric alongside the Nightshade, a growing sense of unease settling in his heart.

The sun was now high in the sky, casting dappled light through the leaves of the trees. Brother Thomas realised that hours had passed since he first set foot on the path. With the clues he had gathered, it was time to return to the village. He had much to contemplate and, he hoped, enough to shed light on the darkness of Elanor's passing.

As he retraced his steps back through Saint Cuthbert's Woods, Brother Thomas felt a weight upon his spirit. The answers he sought were close, he could feel them, but they were tangled in a web of mystery and uncertainty.

Chapter 10: Whispers of Nightshade

The evening had draped itself over the village, casting a cloak of shadows pierced only by the warm glow emanating from the Crooked Ploughman. The hearth fire crackled and spat, a merry dance of flames that seemed to hold the darkness at bay. The inn was abuzz with the low murmur of villagers seeking respite from the day's toils, the clinking of tankards, and an occasional hearty laugh that cut through the din.

Brother Thomas pushed open the heavy oak door, the scent of roasted meat and ale greeting him as he stepped into the inviting warmth. His eyes, scanned the room until they found the innkeeper, a portly man with a ruddy complexion and a ready smile, polishing a row of mugs behind the bar.

"Good eve, ," Brother Thomas greeted as he approached, his voice a gentle rumble.

The inn keeper looked up, his smile broadening. "Brother Thomas! What brings you to my humble establishment this fine night?"

"I seek understanding, and perhaps a bit of ale to warm a man's bones," Brother Thomas replied, easing onto a stool.

The innkeeper poured a generous measure of ale and slid it across the bar. "Understanding, eh? That's a tall order, but I'll do what I can."

Brother Thomas took a small sip, savoring the rich flavor, before he leaned in, his voice lowering. "It's about Mathew, the blacksmith. I've been told he had a lover before his heart was ensnared by dear Elanor."

The inn keeper's eyes darted around the room before he leaned in, matching Brother Thomas's conspiratorial tone. "Aye, that he did. Agnes, the herbalist's apprentice. A quiet lass, kept to herself mostly, but there was a fire in her, especially when it came to Mathew."

"A fire that burnt out?"

The inn keeper nodded. "Like a candle in a storm. Mathew, he's a good man, but when Elanor came to town, it's like he was bewitched. Couldn't see past her, and poor Agnes was left in the cold."

Brother Thomas's brow furrowed. "And her skills... they included the crafting of tinctures and potions, I presume?"

"Indeed," The inn keeper confirmed, his voice a whisper. "She learned from Peter the herbalist, knows her way around a mortar and pestle. Why, she could cure a cough with honey and thyme, or ease a fever with willow bark."

"And nightshade?" Brother Thomas pressed, his eyes intent.

The inn keeper's hand stilled on the mug he was cleaning, his expression turning grave. "Aye, that too. But she's no fool. Knows the danger it holds. Why do you ask?"

Brother Thomas's gaze was steady, heavy with unspoken knowledge. "Because, a flower of nightshade was found where Elanor's body was discovered. And now, suspicion grows where once there was none."

The innkeeper's mouth opened slightly, his eyes reflecting the flicker of the hearth. "You think Agnes..."

"I think nothing yet," Brother Thomas interjected softly. "But the path of truth is often twisted, like the vines of nightshade itself. I must tread carefully, for the sake of all involved."

The inn keeper nodded slowly, a mix of concern and intrigue playing across his features. "You'll find no gossip here, Brother. But if there's aught you need to know, I'll help as I can."

"Thank you. Your discretion is a balm to troubled times," Brother Thomas said, finishing his ale and rising from his stool. "Good night to you."

"And to you, Brother," The inn keeper replied.

Chapter 11: Whispers in the Shadows

Brother Thomas approached the modest dwelling of Agnes with a heart laden with purpose and a mind swirling with questions. The sun was dipping low, casting elongated shadows that seemed to reach for him as he walked, as though the day itself were trying to hold him back from the night's grim secrets. The door to Agnes's home was ajar, and a faint light flickered from within, betraying the presence of a solitary candle.

He rapped softly on the wooden frame, his knuckles brushing against the rough-hewn surface. "Agnes, it is Brother Thomas," he called in a gentle tone, meant not to startle. There was a moment's pause, and then the sound of shuffling footsteps approached the door.

Agnes appeared, her face a canvas of worry and grief. "Brother Thomas," she greeted, her voice betraying the strain of untold sorrow. "To what do I owe the honour at this late hour?"

"I am here on a matter most grave," Brother Thomas replied, stepping into the humble abode as Agnes motioned him inside. "It concerns the tragic passing of Elanor.."

A gasp escaped Agnes's lips, and she quickly crossed herself, her eyes casting down. "May the Lord have mercy on her soul," she whispered. "Please, take a seat," she gestured to a wooden stool by the dying fire.

Brother Thomas sat, his gaze never leaving Agnes as she settled across from him, her hands clasped tightly in her lap. "I must ask you some difficult questions," he began, his voice soft yet firm. "It is known that Elanor and Matthew, the blacksmith, had intentions to leave this place together. You, being close to Matthew, might hold knowledge that could shed light upon her untimely death."

Agnes's eyes flickered with a complex emotion, and for a moment, Brother Thomas thought he saw a shadow of fear pass through them. "I know not of what you speak," she said, her voice a mere whisper. "Matthew's heart belonged to Elanor, and mine... mine has long accepted that."

"Yet, acceptance does not always mean absence of knowledge," Brother Thomas pressed gently. "Did Matthew ever confide in you about their plans? Or perhaps, did Elanor reach out to you before her demise?"

Agnes hesitated, a tremor in her breath. "Elanor... she was a kind soul," she began, her voice gaining strength. "She came to me the day before she... before she was found. She was frightened, Brother Thomas. She spoke of a secret, something she had discovered that put fear into her heart."

"A secret?" Brother Thomas leaned forward, his attention sharpening. "Did she speak of what it was?"

"She mentioned not, but she intended to tell Matthew on the morrow," Agnes said, her eyes now fixed on the dying embers of the fire. "She never got the chance. The next we knew, she was found in Saint Cuthbert's woods, lifeless and cold."

Brother Thomas absorbed her words, a sense of urgency growing within him. "Did anyone else know of her visit to you? Anyone who might have seen her leave or held ill will against her?"

Agnes shook her head slowly. "The streets were empty, as if the very air held its breath. But she spoke of a shadow that followed her, one she could not see but felt in her very soul."

"A shadow," Brother Thomas echoed, his mind racing with the implications. "We must find out more about this shadow, for it may lead us to the truth of Elanor's fate."

Agnes nodded solemnly. "I will help in any way I can, Brother Thomas. Elanor deserved a life of happiness, not the cruel death that befell her."

Chapter 12: Revelations in the Infirmary

Brother Thomas made his way through the quiet halls of the infirmary, the scent of healing herbs and the soft murmur of prayers filling the air. His heart was heavy with the weight of the secrets that had been unearthed, and he sought solace in the familiar presence of Matthew, the blacksmith, who lay in a dimly lit chamber, his form still and pale against the crisp white linens.

As Brother Thomas approached, he found Matthew's eyes fixed on the window, his gaze distant and troubled. "Matthew," Brother Thomas called out softly, his voice a gentle balm in the hushed confines of the infirmary.

The blacksmith turned to face him, his eyes shadowed with weariness. "Brother Thomas," he greeted, his voice faltering with the weight of unspoken grief.

"I have come to check on your well-being and to share with you the discoveries that have been made in our pursuit of truth," Brother Thomas said, taking a seat by Matthew's bedside.

Matthew's brow furrowed in curiosity, and he nodded for Brother Thomas to continue.

"It has come to light that Eleanor was haunted by a shadow in her final days, a presence that filled her with fear and foreboding," Brother Thomas explained. "Agnes has spoken of it, and it seems that this shadow may hold the key to understanding the circumstances of her untimely death."

Matthew's eyes widened with a flicker of recognition, and he spoke in a voice tinged with uncertainty. "Brother Thomas, I know not what this shadow may be, but I swear to aid you in uncovering the truth."

As they delved deeper into their conversation, Brother Thomas felt a sense of kinship with Matthew, a shared determination to bring justice to Eleanor's memory. Yet, as they spoke, a thought began to unfurl in Brother Thomas's mind, a thread of connection between the shadow that had haunted Eleanor and the origins of Matthew's own lineage.

"Matthew, I have a question of great import," Brother Thomas began, his voice taking on a note of urgency. "Tell me of your family, of your roots in this village."

Matthew's expression grew pensive, and he spoke with a tinge of sorrow. "I am an only child, and my parents reside in the village. They originally came from the South Lands, where the nightshade grows in abundance."

Brother Thomas's eyes widened in realization, a surge of understanding coursing through him. "The South Lands, where the art of herbalism is revered," he mused. "And your father, was he not once an apprentice to a renowned herbalist in those lands?"

Matthew's gaze sharpened with surprise, and he nodded slowly. "Aye, my father did speak of his time as an apprentice in the South Lands. But what does this have to do with the shadow that plagued Eleanor?"

"Nightshade," Brother Thomas murmured, his mind racing with the implications. "The South Lands are known for their potent herbs and the secrets they hold. Nightshade, in particular, is a plant steeped in mystery and darkness. Could it be that the shadow that haunted Eleanor is somehow tied to the secrets of your family's origins?"

Matthew's eyes widened with a dawning realization, and he spoke in a voice tinged with uncertainty. "Brother Thomas, I know not what dark forces may be at play, but I swear to aid you in uncovering the truth. If there is a connection between my family's past and the shadow that haunted Eleanor, we must bring it to light."

As Brother Thomas and Matthew delved deeper into the enigma that had woven itself into the fabric of their lives, a sense of purpose and resolve enveloped them, binding them in a shared quest to unravel the mysteries that had cast their world into turmoil.

Chapter 13: A Herbalist's Tale.

Brother Thomas had always been fascinated by the history of the people in the village. He loved to hear the stories of how families had come to settle in the area, and the traditions and skills they had brought with them. So when he heard that Mathew's father, Peter, had originally come from the south lands and had been apprenticed to a herbalist, he knew he had to visit them to learn more. As he made his way to their humble cottage on the outskirts of the village, Brother Thomas couldn't help but feel a sense of excitement. As he approached the cottage, he could see Peter and Maude working in their small garden. "Good day," Peter called out as he spotted the monk approaching. "What brings you to our humble abode?" "I have spoken to Mathew in the infirmary, and he has told me about your background and the skills you brought with you from the south lands," Brother Thomas replied with a warm smile. Peter and Maude exchanged a knowing look before inviting Brother Thomas into their home. As they sat around the small table, Peter began to recount the story of how he had been apprenticed to a renowned herbalist in the south lands. He had spent years learning the art of healing and the properties of various plants and herbs. "Eventually, I felt the call to seek out my own path and make a new home for myself," he added, his eyes sparkling with fond memories. "And so, I made the long journey to this village, where I found a place to settle and continue my work as a herbalist." Brother Thomas listened intently as Peter spoke, feeling a deep sense of admiration for Peter and the knowledge he had acquired. As they continued to talk, Peter revealed that it was in the village that he had met Maude and had fallen in love with her. They had soon become betrothed, and a year later, Mathew had been born. "Maude has always had a natural affinity for the plants and herbs," Peter said with pride. "She has been my greatest apprentice and has learned so much over the years." As he bid Peter and Maude farewell and made his way back to the village, he couldn't help but ponder. He knew that Peter or Maude could have used their knowledge and skills to murder Elanor, but what reason did they have?

Chapter 14: The Narrowing of Suspects

Brother Thomas sat in the small, dimly lit room of the Crooked Ploughman he had been poring over the evidence for days, and finally, he had narrowed down the list of suspects to three: Agnes, Peter, and Maude.

All three had the herbalist skills to poison Eleanor with the deadly nightshade plant, but only Agnes had a motive. Agnes, the village healer, had been jealous of Elanor.

But Brother Thomas believed Agnes when she said that she only wished Matthew and Elanor well. That left Peter and Maude as his main suspects.

He decided to start with Peter. As he made his way to Peter and Maude's cottage, he couldn't shake the feeling that he was getting closer to the truth. The air was heavy with the scent of nightshade, and the sound of the wind rustling through the trees seemed to whisper secrets to him.

When he arrived at the cottage, he found the herbalist working in his garden, tending to his various plants and herbs. Peter looked up as Brother Thomas approached, his face etched with lines of worry and exhaustion.

"Peter, I need to speak with you again," Brother Thomas said, his voice firm and unwavering.

Peter nodded and led Brother Thomas into his cottage, where they sat at a small wooden table. Brother Thomas studied Peter's face, searching for any sign of guilt or deceit.

"I need to know the truth," Brother Thomas said. "Did you have anything to do with Elanor's death?"

Peter's eyes widened in shock, and he shook his head vehemently. "I swear on my life, I had nothing to do with it. I would never harm Elanor. She was a kind and gentle soul, and I would never do anything to hurt her."

Brother Thomas studied Peter's face carefully, searching for any hint of deception. But all he saw was genuine concern and anguish.

"Peter, where is Maude? I need to speak with her as well," Brother Thomas asked, looking around the garden. "She's gone into the village for supplies and won't be back until later," Peter replied, knowing that Thomas needed to talk to Maude as well. "I'll let her know that you're looking for her when she gets back," Peter added,

Brother Thomas thanked Peter for his time and left the cottage, feeling uncertain and frustrated. As he made his way back to the tavern, Brother Thomas couldn't shake the feeling that he was missing something crucial. He needed to find the truth, for the sake of Elanor and for the sake of justice. With a determined set to his jaw, he vowed to continue his investigation until he uncovered the truth, no matter how long it took.

Chapter 15: The Truth Unveiled

The next day, as the sun began to set over the horizon, Brother Thomas made his way back to the quaint cottage where Maude lived. He found her sitting alone by the fireplace, her eyes filled with a mixture of fear and guilt.

"Maude, I need to speak with you again," Brother Thomas said, his voice gentle but firm.

Maude looked up at him with sharp, suspicious eyes, but she nodded and gestured for him to sit.

"Maude, I need to know the truth," Brother Thomas said. "Did you have anything to do with Elanor's death?"

Maude's heart raced as she met Brother Thomas' gaze. her eyes narrowed, and she knew she could no longer hide the truth that had been weighing heavily on her conscience. With a heavy sigh, she finally spoke, her voice barely above a whisper.

"Yes, Brother Thomas. I... I had a hand in Elanor's death," Maude confessed, her eyes brimming with tears. "When Peter and I became betrothed, I was already carrying another man's child. Baron Geoffrey was my lover, and I kept it a secret from everyone, including Peter."

Brother Thomas listened in stunned silence as Maude's confession unfolded before him. The pieces of the puzzle were finally starting to come together, revealing a web of deceit and betrayal that had been carefully woven over the years.

"Everything was fine until my son, Mathew, fell in love with Elanor," Maude continued, her voice trembling with emotion. "I had to tell Elanor the truth, that both she and Mathew were Geoffrey's children and could never be together. Elanor had planned to reveal the truth to Mathew, and I... I couldn't let that happen."

She arrived at the cottage, the day she and Mathew had planned to run away together, she couldn't shake the guilt of keeping the truth from him. She poured out her heart, confessing her love for Mathew but also her fear of losing him if she told him the truth. I listened intently and then gave her some spiced wine, assuring her that it would calm her nerves. She set off to meet Mathew, but felt increasingly dizzy and disoriented. I followed her, and when she reached the woods,she collapsed on the ground. As she drifted into darkness I rushed to her side, begged for her forgiveness the spiced wine I had given her was made from the deadly nightshade plant. As Mathew approached, I crept up behind him and knocked him unconscious, determined to keep him from finding Elanor before she succumbed to the poison.

Tears streamed down Maude's face as she recounted the events that had led to Elanor's tragic death. The weight of her guilt and sorrow was almost unbearable, but she knew she had to face the consequences of her actions.

Her voice barely audible. "I thought I was protecting my family, but I only brought more pain and suffering upon us all."

Brother Thomas placed a comforting hand on Maude's shoulder, his eyes filled with compassion and understanding. "Maude, what you did was wrong, but I believe that true repentance and redemption are still possible," he said softly. "Together, we will seek forgiveness and make amends for the mistakes of the past."

Maude, her hands trembling as she gripped the edge of the table, knew that this was the moment she had been dreading. "It's too late for redemption, Brother Thomas, Once the truth is out, I can never face Peter or Mathew again. They will never forgive me for what I've done, and I can't bear to live with the guilt and shame any longer."

With that, Maude reached into the pocket of her gown and pulled out a small vial of nightshade poison, the last remnants of the deadly concoction she had used to poison Elanor. Without hesitation, she unscrewed the cap and raised the vial to her lips, swallowing the bitter liquid in one swift motion.

As the poison took hold of her body, Maude felt a sense of peace wash over her, knowing that soon her suffering would be at an end. She closed her eyes and whispered to Brother Thomas " Pray for me" before slipping into unconsciousness, her final breath coming in a soft, whispered sigh.

And in that moment, Maude knew that she had made her choice, and there was no turning back. Her fate was sealed, and she would soon be free from the burden of her sins forevermore.

Chapter 16: Facing the Shadows of the Past.

As the sun began to rise over the village, a somber gathering took place at the cottage where Maude lived. Peter, Maude's husband, Mathew, her son, Baron Geoffrey, and Lord Edmund, Elanor's betrothed, had all been summoned to hear the truth surrounding Elanor's tragic death.

Brother Thomas stood before them, his expression grave yet filled with compassion. He recounted Maude's confession, detailing the events that had led to the heartbreaking loss of Elanor.

Peter's eyes widened in shock as he heard the truth about Maude's past with Baron Geoffrey and the secret she had kept hidden for so long. His heart ached with a mixture of betrayal and understanding, knowing that the woman he loved had carried such a heavy burden all these years.

Mathew, his face pale with guilt and remorse, the weight of his actions and the consequences they had brought upon their family weighed heavily on his young shoulders.

Baron Geoffrey listened in silence, his face a mask of sorrow and regret. He had never imagined that his past indiscretions would come back to haunt him in such a tragic way, tearing apart the lives of those he held dear.

Lord Edmund, Elanor's betrothed, stood with a heavy heart, his grief for his lost love mingling with a sense of betrayal and confusion. The truth had shattered the image he had held of Elanor and the future they had planned together.

As Brother Thomas finished recounting the events that had unfolded, a heavy silence descended upon the room. Each person grappled with their own emotions, trying to make sense of the tangled web of lies and deceit that had been woven around them.

Finally, Peter stepped forward, his voice filled with a mix of pain and forgiveness.

"I may never fully understand the choices she made, but we must now all live with the consequences."

Mathew bowed his head, tears streaming down his face. "I am so sorry, Father," he whispered, his voice filled with remorse. "I never meant for any of this to happen."

Baron Geoffrey and Lord Edmund exchanged a solemn nod, their hearts heavy with the weight of the truth that had been revealed. They knew that forgiveness would not come easily, but they were willing to take the first steps.

As the sun rose higher in the sky, casting a warm glow over the gathered group, a sense of hope filled the air. The path ahead would be long and difficult, but with honesty, humility, and a willingness to face the truth, they knew that they could overcome the shadows of the past and move forward together.

Sam Wade and the strange Case of Eleanor Grimlore

Chapter 1: The Dark Web

Sam Wade trudged through the dimly lit streets of Nightshade City, his worn-out trench coat flapping in the cool autumn breeze. He let out a heavy sigh as he reached the towering building that housed the Paranormal Police Department. As one of the few detectives on the force, Sam's days were always filled with strange and supernatural cases. But tonight, another sinister mystery awaited him.

Within the precinct's ancient walls, Sam made his way past flickering candles and floating orbs of light that illuminated the long hallway. The air was thick with the scent of incense, mingling with the faint aroma of potions and mystical herbs. The twenty-first century world had long abandoned technology, embracing the power of magic instead.

Sam's office, tucked away on the top floor, was adorned with a clutter of enchanted artifacts, dusty grimoires, and crystal orbs. His desk was strewn with parchment and quills, rather than computers and tablets. As he settled into his creaky chair, the sound of footsteps echoed through the hallway, growing louder as they approached his office.

The door swung open, revealing a tall figure cloaked in shadows. It was his superior, Captain Alexandria Nightshade, her piercing blue eyes gleaming with determination. She handed Sam a thick file, the name "Eleanor Grimlore" etched boldly across the cover.

"Sam, we've got a serious situation on our hands," Captain Nightshade said, her voice laced with urgency. "Eleanor Grimlore, a society debutante, was found strangled in her bathtub on Halloween night, and I need you to lead the investigation."

Sam's eyebrows furrowed in concern as he skimmed through the file. Eleanor Grimlore was known for her extravagant parties and influential connections. Her death threatened to shake the foundations of Nightshade City's elite social circles.

"I want you to find out who did this, Sam," Captain Nightshade continued firmly. "The city needs answers. With your unique blend of magic and detective skills, I trust you'll uncover the truth."

Sam nodded, his mind already racing with possibilities. He was no stranger to the shadowy underbelly of Nightshade City, the dark magic that lurked beneath the glimmering surface. But this case felt different. There was an air of malevolence, a sinister presence that sent chills down his spine.

As he stepped out into the night once again, the moon cast an eerie glow on the cobblestone streets. Sam knew the path ahead would be treacherous, filled with magic and secrets that could bring down even the bravest. Yet he also knew that he had a duty to the city and to the memory of Eleanor Grimlore.

Drawing on his own magic, Sam conjured a swirling blue orb that illuminated the way ahead. With every step, the darkness seemed to grow denser, the stakes higher. Sam Wade, a detective in a world fueled by magic, was about to face his most challenging investigation yet.

Chapter 2: Secrets Unveiled

Sam Wade stood outside the grand apartment building that housed Eleanor Grimlore's lavish residence. The moon hung high in the starless night sky as he muttered an incantation, unlocking the sealed entrance. Stepping inside, he was met with an opulent foyer adorned with magical tapestries and shimmering chandeliers. The air was tinged with a faint aroma of roses, intermingled with a sullen heaviness. Sam took a deep breath, preparing himself for the chilling secrets that lay within.

Ascending the plush, carpeted staircase, Sam reached the door to Eleanor's apartment. As he approached, a prickle of magic brushed against his senses, a residue left by the powerful enchantments that surrounded her living quarters.

He pushed open the door, finding himself in a room drowned in darkness, the moonlight struggling to penetrate the heavy curtains. Sam' wand glowed softly, casting a radiant glow around the room.

Carefully, he began to inspect every inch of the scene. His keen eyes spotted an overturned vase, shattered near the entrance. A hint of dried blood adorned the shards, suggesting that Eleanor had put up a fight. The bathroom door stood ajar, and Sam felt a chill crawling up his spine as he approached.

Inside the dimly lit bathroom, he saw the psychic impression of the lifeless body, still lying in the bathtub. Eleanor Grimlore's once-beautiful face was now marred by the signs of a brutal struggle. Her normally vibrant red hair was disheveled and matted, and the marks of strangulation were evident on her neck.

Stepping away, Sam's eyes landed on Poison Ivy, Eleanor's maid, who stood in the doorway, her eyes swollen with tears. Ivy was a witch who possessed a deep connection to the earthly elements, often seen tending to Eleanor's extensive garden.

"Poison Ivy," Sam spoke softly, "I'm Detective Sam Wade. I need to ask you a few questions about the night of the murder."

Ivy trembled, her hands clutching her apron nervously. "I... I'll help in any way I can," she stammered. "But I can't believe Eleanor's gone. She was like family to me."

Sam nodded sympathetically, his gaze shifting between the devastated maid and Eleanor's lifeless body. "Tell me about the party, Ivy. Who attended and what happened?"

Ivy bit her trembling lip before recounting the details. "It was a Halloween soiree Detective. The Grimlores always held extravagant gatherings, and Eleanor's party was no different. There were quite a few notable figures in attendance, including Lord Ravenwood, a powerful sorcerer, and Lady Astrid, a renowned enchantress. The party lasted well into the night, but I retired to my quarters before midnight. The last time I saw Eleanor was when she entered her room to prepare for bed."

Sam furrowed his brow, processing the information. "Did anything stand out to you that night? Anyone acting strangely or exhibiting hostile behavior?"

Ivy hesitated, her eyes clouded with uncertainty. "There was something unsettling about Lord Ravenwood's demeanor. I couldn't quite put my finger on it, but he seemed agitated and his usual charm was absent. Eleanor and he had exchanged a few tense words during the evening."

Sam took note of the potential lead. Lord Ravenwood's involvement in such a high-profile murder case could have dire consequences for the magical community. Determined to uncover the truth, Sam thanked Poison Ivy for her cooperation and assured her that justice would be served.

As Sam left the apartment, he knew the investigation had only just begun. The twisted web of motives and magical mischief lay before him, and he was determined to catch the perpetrator before they could strike again. With Poison Ivy's words echoing in his mind, Sam delved deeper into the shadowy secrets of Nightshade City, his magic-infused investigation threatening to unravel the very fabric of the supernatural world.

Chapter 3: Shadows of Suspicion

Sam Wade made his way through the dimly lit streets of Nightshade City, his thoughts consumed by the mysteries surrounding Eleanor Grimelore's murder. Lord Ravenwood's eerie presence at the Halloween party had piqued Sam's curiosity, and he knew that confronting the powerful sorcerer could lead to vital information.

Arriving at Lord Ravenwood's mansion, Sam was greeted by an imposing wrought-iron gate, adorned with intricately woven spells of protection. Without hesitation, he raised his wand and recited the counter-incantation, causing the gate to swing open with a loud creak.

Passing through the meticulously manicured garden, Sam made his way to the grand entrance. The colossal wooden doors parted, revealing a spacious foyer dominated by an ornate chandelier that bathed the room in a soft, ethereal glow. Lord Ravenwood, a tall figure draped in midnight black robes, emerged from the shadows.

"Detective Wade," Lord Ravenwood greeted, his voice a smooth velvet that sent shivers down Sam's spine. "To what do I owe this unexpected visit?"

Sam locked eyes with the sorcerer, his gaze unwavering. "Lord Ravenwood, I'm here to inquire about the night of Eleanor Grimelore's murder. I have reason to believe that you may have information relevant to the investigation."

The sorcerer raised an eyebrow, his dark eyes narrowing with intrigue. "Ah, Eleanor. She was a fascinating woman, Detective. We had known each other for many years, our paths often intertwined due to our shared magical pursuits."

Sam leaned forward, his voice firm. "What was the nature of your relationship with Eleanor, Lord Ravenwood?"

A faint smile danced across Ravenwood's lips, his eyes hinting at hidden emotions. "We were once close, Detective. But as time went on, our paths diverged, leading to a strained connection."

Sam pressed further. "And what about the argument you had with Eleanor at her Halloween party? Can you shed some light on that?"

Lord Ravenwood's expression darkened, a flicker of annoyance crossing his face. "It was merely a disagreement, detective. Eleanor and I saw things differently when it came to magic, our ideologies clashing like thunder and lightning. The argument grew heated, and I chose to leave the party, seeking solace elsewhere."

Sam absorbed Lord Ravenwood's words, sensing there was more beneath the surface. "Is there anyone who can corroborate your alibi, someone who can vouch for your whereabouts after leaving the party?"

A moment of uncertainty flashed across Ravenwood's face, quickly replaced by a composed facade. "No, Detective. I decided to spend the rest of the evening in solitude, reflecting on our exchange."

Sam ended the conversation, but Ravenwood's evasiveness only deepened his suspicion. As he left the sorcerer's mansion, the puzzle pieces of Eleanor's murder continued to swirl in his mind.

Back at his office, Sam diligently sifted through the evidence he had gathered so far. The strained relationship between Eleanor Grimelore and Lord Ravenwood echoed like a haunting melody, and Sam knew that exploring this connection further would be crucial. The unresolved argument and the sorcerer's mysterious alibi would demand closer scrutiny.

As he embarked on the next phase of the investigation, Sam couldn't help but feel the shadows of suspicion lurking in the corners of Nightshade City. With every step, the puzzle inched closer to completion, revealing the elusive truth that lay buried beneath layers of clandestine enchantments.

Chapter 4: Tangled Webs

As the sun set over Nightshade City, Sam Wade found himself standing outside Poison Ivy's botanical haven. He knew that her unique insight into the magical underbelly of the city could hold the key to unraveling the mystery behind Eleanor Grimelore's murder. With a determined stride, he approached the door and knocked.

The door creaked open, revealing Poison Ivy's smirking visage. "Well, well, Detective Wade. To what do I owe the pleasure of your visit?" she purred, her voice as smooth as silk.

Sam met her gaze, his eyes searching for any flicker of truth. "Ivy, I need to know more about the argument between Eleanor Grimelore and Lord Ravenwood. Did you witness it?"

Poison Ivy playfully twirled a lock of her verdant hair, a mischievous glint in her emerald eyes. "Why, Detective, what makes you think that I would know anything about their quarrel?"

Sam's voice sharpened. "Don't play games, Ivy. The truth will come out eventually. It's in your best interest to cooperate."

A sly smile played on Poison Ivy's lips as she slowly opened the door, gesturing for Sam to enter. "Very well, Detective. I'll tell you what I know, but you owe me a favor in return."

Sam hesitated for a moment, weighing the cost of her request against the potential reward of information. With a firm resolve, he nodded, sealing the unseen pact.

Poison Ivy led Sam to her private study, a sanctuary of nature's beauty engulfing them as they stepped inside. She settled into an overstuffed leather chair, her eyes filled with knowing. "Lord Ravenwood and Eleanor did argue that night, but it wasn't just about their clashing magical ideologies. There was something more personal fueling their heated exchange."

Sam leaned forward, curiosity burning within him. "What was it, Ivy? What could have driven them to such intensity?"

Poison Ivy leaned back, her voice dripping with intrigue. "It was jealousy, Detective. Lord Ravenwood harbored an intense envy for Eleanor's mastery of forbidden magics. He saw her as a rival, a threat to his own power. Their argument erupted into a storm of words, each one laced with bitter resentment."

Sam absorbed the revelation, the puzzle pieces finally starting to fit. But he knew there was more to uncover. "Ivy, I need to know where Lord Ravenwood went after the argument. Did he leave the party alone, as he claimed?"

A mischievous glimmer sparkled in Poison Ivy's eyes as she revealed her trump card. "Oh, Detective, you'll find this quite interesting. Lord Ravenwood didn't leave the party alone that night. He sought solace in my company, spending the rest of the evening with me."

Sam felt a jolt of shock, the discovery weaving an even thornier path through the investigation. "Are you certain, Ivy? Can anyone vouch for your encounter with Lord Ravenwood?"

Poison Ivy smirked, revealing a knowledge that gleamed like a hidden gem. "Fear not, Detective. There are whispers in the depths of Nightshade City, secrets that intertwine like the roots of an ancient tree. These whispers will provide the evidence you seek."

Sam left Poison Ivy's lair, his mind ablaze with new leads and lingering questions. Life in Nightshade City, it seemed, was entangled in a delicate mesh of alliances and deceptions. As he delved deeper into the web of secrets, the truth took on an elusive form, just out of reach.

Chapter 5: Unveiling Shadows

Determined to unearth more clues about the fateful party where Eleanor Grimelore met her demise, Sam Wade sought out his old friend, Honeysuckle, a gossip columnist for the local newspaper. He knew that Honeysuckle's connections and insider knowledge might shed light on the enigma surrounding the influential attendees.

Sam found Honeysuckle sipping her favorite tea at a quaint cafe, surrounded by a stack of magazines and a notepad bursting with scribbled notes. Her sharp gaze met Sam's as he approached her table. "Well, well, if it isn't my favorite detective. What brings you to my humble abode?"

Sam greeted her with a warm smile. "Honeysuckle, I need your expertise. I'm investigating Eleanor Grimelore's murder, and I'm looking for information on who attended the party."

Honeysuckle raised an eyebrow, a glimmer of mischief in her eyes. "Ah, a juicy story indeed. Lucky for you, my dear friend, I've been keeping tabs on Nightshade City's most influential figures."

Sam leaned in closer, his curiosity piqued. "Tell me, Honeysuckle, who was in attendance? Did anyone unexpected make an appearance?"

Honeysuckle's lips curled into a knowing grin. "Oh, my dear Sam, the guest list was a veritable who's who of the city's power players. And guess who was among them? None other than your own Chief of Police, James Darkwood."

Sam's eyes widened with surprise, the revelation striking him like a bolt of lightning. "Darkwood? Are you sure, Honeysuckle?"

Her gaze never wavered as she confirmed with conviction. "Positive, Sam. Darkwood would not have missed that soiree for the world. He arrived with an air of importance, mingling effortlessly with the elite of Nightshade City."

The implications hung heavy in the air, casting an ominous shadow over Sam's thoughts. Could his own superior be connected to Eleanor's murder? The trust Sam had placed in Darkwood suddenly seemed fragile, like a spider's web clinging precariously to a branch.

Sam's voice betrayed a hint of concern. "Honeysuckle, do you know anything else? Any details that could shed light on James Darkwood's involvement?"

Honeysuckle tapped her pen against her notepad, her expression thoughtful. "Hmm, I can't say for certain, Sam. But rumors have been swirling for some time, whispers of corruption and hidden motives. It might be worth looking deeper into Darkwood's history, his alliances, and any enemies he might have."

Sam absorbed the information, his mind buzzing with possibilities. He thanked Honeysuckle for her insights and left the cafe with newfound determination. Darkwood's presence at the party raised a host of troubling questions, and Sam was resolved to face the truth head-on.

As night fell over Nightshade City, Sam pondered the tangled web woven by Eleanor's murder. Each piece of the puzzle seemed to deepen the shadows, revealing a city rife with secrets and hidden agendas. The path ahead was treacherous, and Sam knew that uncovering the truth might come at a great cost.

Chapter 6: Shadows and Secrets

With Honeysuckle's revelations fresh in his mind, Sam Wade prepared himself for a direct confrontation. He sought an audience with Chief of Police, James Darkwood, eager to confront him about his attendance at the party that fateful night.

Finding Darkwood behind his desk in the dimly lit police station, Sam approached cautiously. The chief looked up from his paperwork, his gaze meeting Sam's with a hint of weariness.

"Chief Darkwood," Sam began, his voice resolute. "I have some questions about the night of Eleanor Grimelore's murder."

Darkwood leaned back in his chair, studying Sam with a mixture of curiosity and consternation. "What's on your mind, Detective Wade? I thought we had covered everything on this case."

Sam's eyes narrowed, his tone firm. "You attended the party, Chief. Can you confirm that?"

Darkwood's expression remained guarded, but he nodded slowly. "Yes, I was there. A guest of Lord Ravenwood, a wealthy benefactor who has been supporting my campaign for mayor of Nightshade City."

Sam's mind churned with the implications of Darkwood's response. The connections between Darkwood, Lord Ravenwood, and the crime at hand grew ever more tangled. A benefactor seeking to secure the chief's loyalty through financial support, could this be the motive behind the murder?

Gathering his thoughts, Sam pressed on. "Chief Darkwood, can you shed any light on the events of that evening? Did you see anything unusual, anyone acting suspiciously?"

Darkwood's gaze turned distant, as if searching his memories. "I can't say I noticed anything out of the ordinary, Sam. It was a gathering of the city's elite, after all. People come and go, navigating their own social agendas."

The chief's evasiveness nudged Sam's instincts further. Was Darkwood deliberately withholding information? Or was he genuinely unaware of the events that unfolded that fateful night?

Sam chose his words carefully, pressing the chief for more. "Did you interact with Eleanor Grimelore that evening? Or witness anyone behaving aggressively towards her?"

Darkwood sighed, his face clouded with a mix of sorrow and frustration. "I hardly knew the woman, Sam. Eleanor and I crossed paths a few times, but nothing more than formalities. As for aggression, well, it's a party like any other. Emotions run high, but nothing out of the ordinary caught my attention."

Sam's suspicion lingered, but he knew he needed more than a hunch. Darkwood's connection to Lord Ravenwood, along with the financial support for his political aspirations, raised questions about the chief's integrity and motives.

Thanking Darkwood for his time, Sam left the office, the weight of uncertainty heavy on his shoulders. As he walked the seemingly endless corridors of the police station, Sam vowed to dig deeper into Lord Ravenwood's involvement and his influence over Darkwood's campaign.

Nightshade City teemed with shadows and secrets, and Sam Wade was determined to shine a light on the truth, no matter the cost.

Chapter 7: Whispers of Alchemy

As Sam delved further into the tangled web of Eleanor Grimelore's life, he stumbled upon a startling revelation. It seemed that Eleanor had emerged onto the social scene of Nightshade City less than three years ago, a woman of mystery and intrigue. She possessed an air of wealth but had no visible means of earning it, no trust fund, shares, or rich parents to lean on.

Intrigued by this new piece of information, Sam sought the counsel of Belladonna, an informant with ears everywhere in the city's underbelly.

He knew Belladonna had her finger on the pulse of rumors and whispered secrets.

Finding her in her secluded den, surrounded by the aroma of exotic herbs and potions, Sam cut straight to the chase. "Belladonna , I need your help. Have you heard anything about Eleanor Grimelore and her sudden wealth?"

Belladonnas emerald eyes gleamed with a mix of intrigue and mischief as she leaned forward, her voice barely above a whisper. "Ah, Eleanor. The talk of the town, she was. It wasn't just her sudden appearance that raised eyebrows, it was the source of her wealth. Rumors circulated that she had stumbled upon the secret that every witch and warlock in Nightshade City coveted."

Sam's curiosity piqued, he leaned in, eager to hear more. "And what secret would that be?"

Belladonnas wicked smile widened. "The secret, my dear detective, of turning base metal into gold. Alchemy. The ancient art that has driven many a sorcerer mad in their pursuit of boundless wealth."

Sam's mind raced with the implications of this revelation. If Eleanor had indeed discovered the secret, she would have possessed a power coveted by many. It explained the sudden influx of wealth and her newfound status in the city's upper echelons. But could this knowledge have led to her demise?

Thanking Belladonna for the information, Sam knew he had to investigate further. He began scouring ancient texts and delving into the history of alchemy, as the answers to Eleanor's murder seemed intricately linked to her rumored discovery.

Days turned into nights as Sam poured over dusty tomes, piecing together fragments of information like a puzzle. Dangerous alchemical formulas, spellbound scrolls, and tales of deceit filled his waking hours.

As the investigation unfolded, Sam began to wonder who might have killed Eleanor. Did someone covet her knowledge, seeking to claim the power of alchemy for themselves? Or was it possible that Eleanor's sudden wealth had attracted the attention of a more sinister force, an entity lurking within the shadows of Nightshade City?

With more questions than answers, Sam Wade pushed forward, determined to uncover the truth, and the person responsible for snuffing out the light of Eleanor Grimlore.

Chapter 8: The Tangled Web of Finances

As Sam dug deeper into the investigation surrounding Eleanor Grimelore's murder, a new thread started to unravel before him. The whispers of alchemy still lingered, but now he wondered if the motive for her killing was purely financial.

Suspecting a possible connection, Sam turned his attention to James Darkwood, the Chief of Police, a charismatic and ambitious man, running a campaign to become the next mayor, and Lord Ravenwood, a man of influence and power, who seemed to have an unusual interest in supporting Darkwood's bid.

Curiosity gnawed at Sam's mind as he delved into the financial accounts of these two men. It was there that he discovered a startling truth. Lord Ravenwood had been transferring an exorbitant amount of money into Darkwood's campaign funds every month.

The sums were unsustainable, far beyond what a typical political campaign would require. It begged the question: why was Ravenwood pouring such a vast fortune into Darkwood's bid for mayor?

The more he uncovered, the clearer the picture became. Darkwood's campaign had become heavily reliant on Ravenwood's financial support. It seemed that Ravenwood had a vested interest in seeing Darkwood ascend to the mayoral position, but the motives behind this alliance remained shrouded in mystery.

Could it be possible that Eleanor Grimelore stumbled upon this dubious financial arrangement? Had she uncovered a secret that threatened to shatter Darkwood's dreams of becoming mayor? Or was there something even more sinister concealed within the shadowed depths of these financial dealings?

With each new revelation, the complexity of the case grew. Sam could sense the pieces coming together, forming a clearer picture of the forces at play in Nightshade City. But how would he unravel this intricate web of lies and deceit? The answers lay buried in the hearts of those with their eyes set on power and the spectre of greed.

Chapter 9: Unveiling the Shadows

Sam's heart skipped a beat as he received a message from his dear friend, Honeysuckle, the renowned gossip columnist of Nightshade City. Intrigued by the prospect of fresh information, he hastened to meet her.

The two met in a secluded corner of a quaint tea shop, escaping the prying eyes and ears of the ever-watchful city. Honeysuckle couldn't contain her excitement as she shared what she had discovered about the fateful argument between Eleanor Grimelore and Lord Ravenwood.

"It had nothing to do with the forbidden arts, Sam," Honeysuckle revealed in a hushed voice. "The argument was rooted in a clandestine affair involving Lord Ravenwood and none other than Police Chief James Darkwood."

Sam's eyebrows shot up in surprise. A scandalous affair involving two influential figures could have far-reaching consequences, providing a motive that twisted through the intricate network of secrets and desires.

Honeysuckle leaned closer, her eyes glimmering with excitement. "But that's not all, my dear Sam. The argument took place in the presence of Lady Morticia Blackwood, the influential socialite known for her razor-sharp wit and connections. She holds a key to unraveling the secrets that lie within the heart of this murder mystery."

Sam leaned back, absorbing the weight of this revelation. A complex tangle of relationships had emerged, intertwining Lord Ravenwood, James Darkwood, and Lady Morticia Blackwood. Their hidden dalliances and possible betrayals posed a new dimension to Eleanor's murder.

Realizing the gravity of the situation, Sam made a mental note to approach Lady Morticia Blackwood discreetly. Her knowledge of the argument could hold vital clues to Eleanor's untimely demise.

Fueled by curiosity and a desire for justice, Sam delved deeper into the backgrounds of those involved. He knew that uncovering the truth required navigating treacherous paths, where loyalties blurred and allegiances shifted like shadows in the night.

As he pieced together the puzzle, Sam couldn't help but wonder about the potential implications. How far would these revelations reach? And would they lead him closer to unmasking the true culprit behind Eleanor's murder?

With new leads in hand and the influence of forbidden magic falling to the wayside, Sam was determined to follow the threads of these complicated relationships. The truth was within reach, but so too were the dangers that awaited him in the murky depths of Nightshade City.

Chapter 10: Shadows of Betrayal

Sam's footsteps echoed against the polished marble floors as he approached the grand manor of Lady Morticia Blackwood. It was time to seek answers, to untangle the web of secrets and lies surrounding the murder of Eleanor Grimelore, and the key lay within the depths of Lady Morticia's knowledge.

The ornate double doors creaked open, revealing a woman of grace and poise standing before him. Lady Morticia's piercing gaze held a mix of intrigue and caution as she welcomed Sam into her lavish abode.

"Mr. Wade," she said, her voice tinged with a hint of curiosity. "To what do I owe the pleasure of your visit today?"

Sam returned her gaze, his eyes determined yet respectful. "Lady Morticia, I've come seeking your wisdom. I've learned that you were present during the argument between Eleanor Grimelore and Lord Ravenwood. Please, shed light on what transpired that day."

Lady Morticia's lips curled into a mix of amusement and sorrow. "Ah, the secrets of the elites, Mr. Wade. Yes, there was an argument indeed, but it had naught to do with dark magic. It was about Lord Ravenwood's lover, the esteemed Police Chief James Darkwood."

Sam's eyes widened in realization. The puzzle pieces fitting together, revealing a hidden world of love and betrayal intertwined with this murder.

Lady Morticia continued, her voice filled with a touch of sadness. "It was a well-known secret among Lord Ravenwood's intimate circles that he preferred the company of men. Society may turn a blind eye to such inclinations, but when passions and emotions collide, consequences can be dire."

Sam's mind raced, connecting the dots. The argument between Eleanor and Lord Ravenwood wasn't rooted in magic at all, but in the shattered trust and broken hearts caused by a forbidden love affair.

"It seems, Lady Morticia, that this love affair may hold the key to Eleanor's murder," Sam remarked, his voice calm but filled with determination.

Lady Morticia nodded, her eyes glimmering with a mix of sorrow and resolve. "Indeed, Mr. Wade. When love and secrets intertwine, darkness can cloud even the brightest of souls. But be cautious, for delving further into this tangled web may uncover more shadows and betrayals than you can possibly imagine."

Sam thanked Lady Morticia for her honesty and took his leave, his mind brimming with new information and unanswered questions. The revelation of Lord Ravenwood's preferences shed a new light on the motives behind Eleanor's murder, and Sam realised that the road ahead would be treacherous.

With resolute determination, Sam vowed to uncover the truth and bring justice to Eleanor Grimelore. Each step taken would bring him closer to unraveling the webs of deceit, even if it meant confronting the darkness that lurked within the hearts of the city's most influential figures.

Chapter 11: Campaign of Concealment

Sam's mind buzzed with newfound knowledge as he scrutinized the information he had gathered. Poison Ivy's alibi had crumbled before his eyes, revealing a sinister connection between Lord Ravenwood and the Police Chief, James Darkwood.

Determined to uncover the truth, Sam set his sights on Lord Ravenwood, aware that confronting him about his whereabouts on the night of the murder could potentially lead to a breakthrough in the case.

Sam tracked down Lord Ravenwood in his opulent study, adorned with grand bookshelves and exquisite art. The pungent scent of aged leather and the soft glow of candlelight created an atmosphere of mystery and secrecy.

"Lord Ravenwood," Sam began, his voice steady but carrying an air of urgency. "I have reason to believe that your alibi, courtesy of Poison Ivy, may be a clever deception. It seems that you spent the night with someone else entirely."

A flicker of panic flashed across Lord Ravenwood's polished facade. He tried to maintain his composure, but Sam could see the cracks forming in his carefully constructed mask.

"You have it all wrong, Mr. Wade," Lord Ravenwood replied, his tone laced with deceit. "I assure you, my whereabouts on that night were entirely accounted for."

Sam narrowed his eyes, refusing to succumb to Lord Ravenwood's manipulative tactics. "I have evidence that suggests otherwise. Let me be plain, Lord Ravenwood. Did you spend the night with James Darkwood, the Police Chief?"

A combination of anger and fear washed over Lord Ravenwood's face, and he was unable to hide the truth any longer. His voice quivered slightly as he responded, "Yes, it is true. James and I were together that night. But please, you must understand, this cannot become public knowledge."

Sam leaned forward, intent on unraveling the web of deceit. "Why were you so intent on keeping this secret? It's evident that your support for James Darkwood's mayoral campaign is tied to this."

Lord Ravenwood's voice wavered as he spoke, "You see, Mr. Wade, our relationship is frowned upon by those in power. I have been supporting James's campaign, and any revelation of our liaison would undermine his chances. It's a delicate situation, one that both of us stand to lose everything over."

Sam absorbed the weight of the confession. The boundaries of love, politics, and murder blurred together, entangling the lives of those involved. He knew that this revelation could shake the very core of Nightshade City's hierarchy, leaving no stone unturned in his quest for justice.

"I understand the complexity of your situation, Lord Ravenwood," Sam said, his voice filled with resolve. "But I'm afraid that the truth cannot remain hidden. Eleanor's murder should not be overshadowed by secrets and manipulation. It's time to face the consequences of your actions."

As Sam left Lord Ravenwood's study, the weight of the investigation grew heavier. The revelation of Lord Ravenwood's clandestine affair brought new challenges and propelled the case to unexpected heights. Sam was prepared to navigate the treacherous path ahead, knowing that uncovering the truth would bring justice to Eleanor Grimelore and reshape the destiny of Nightshade City.

Chapter 12: Tangled Webs Unraveled

Sam couldn't shake off the intriguing connection between Poison Ivy and Lord Ravenwood's. Determined to dig deeper into their twisted webs, he decided to seek answers from Honey Suckle, his ever reliable informant.

Finding Honey Suckle tucked away in a dimly lit booth at a local coffee shop, Sam approached with a mix of anticipation and caution. As the doorbell tinkled, signaling his entrance, Honey Suckle looked up, her eyes sparkling with familiarity.

"Honey, I need your help," Sam began, sitting across from her. "I've uncovered some unsettling information regarding Lord Ravenwood's and his ties to James Darkwood's campaign."

Honey Suckle leaned forward, her voice hushed, "I will tell you what I know, Sam?"

Honeysuckle recounted what she had learned so far: Lord Ravenwood's inability to independently finance James Darkwood's campaign, his arrangement of a loan through Walter Weasley, and that Poison Ivy was initially intended to provide the funds but had backed out on the very day of Eleanor's murder.

Sam brows furrowed as he listened intently, his thoughts weaving together the pieces of the puzzle. After a brief moment of contemplation, honeysuckle leaned closer and whispered, "Sam, I might have something more for you. Walter Weasley owes me a favor. Let me see if I can gather more information."

Grateful for Honey Suckle's assistance, Sam awaited her return. Days turned into an anxious wait until finally, Honey Suckle resurfaced, a sense of urgency in her eyes.

"Sam, I found out what you needed to know," she said, her voice hushed yet filled with purpose. "Walter confirmed that Poison Ivy was indeed set to finance James Darkwood's campaign through Lord Ravenwood. However, something happened, something that made Poison Ivy suddenly pull out of the arrangement on the very day Eleanor was murdered."

Sam leaned forward, his curiosity piqued. "Do you know why she backed out?"

Honey Suckle nodded. "She was unable to provide the money for the loan". Sam's mind whirred with new possibilities, his gaze focused and determined. "It seems that our dear Poison Ivy might know more about Eleanor's murder than she's letting on. I need to pay her a visit."

Honey Suckle nodded in agreement. "But Sam, be careful. She's a master manipulator, and she'll do whatever it takes to protect herself."

Sam's resolve hardened as he stood up, his mind set on the next step in his investigation. "I won't let her elude justice, Honey. I owe it to Eleanor and to this city to uncover the truth."

With Honey Suckle's invaluable information fueling his determination, Sam set out to confront Poison Ivy. The path to justice now seemed within reach, but as he walked out the door, he couldn't shake the feeling that the most treacherous revelations were yet to come.

Chapter 13: Unmasking the Poisonous Scheme

Sam Wade couldn't believe his ears his investigative instincts told him he had stumbled upon a crucial breakthrough. Determined to uncover the truth, he set out to confront Poison Ivy and bring justice to Eleanor's memory.

With a mix of anxiety and anticipation, Sam found himself standing outside Poison Ivy's humble cottage . He strode through the front doors, resolute in his mission to expose the dark secrets lurking within. As he made his way down the hallway, Sam's mind raced with the pieces of the puzzle falling into place. The missing alibi pointed directly at Poison Ivy as the prime suspect in Eleanor's murder. He couldn't help but feel a surge of adrenaline, knowing that he was inching closer to unraveling the truth.

Finally, Sam reached Poison Ivy's secluded study. The room exuded an air of calculated charm, a reflection of its mysterious occupant. Poison Ivy sat composed behind a mahogany desk, a subtle smirk playing on her lips. The anticipation between them was palpable, crackling with tension.

Summoning all his courage, Sam confronted her. He laid out the evidence before her, connecting each dotted line to reveal her motive and her twisted plot. Poison Ivy, driven by her insatiable desire for power and control, confessed to Eleanor's murder without hesitation.

Her words dripped with both arrogance and desperation as she explained her true intentions. Poison Ivy coveted the secret of turning base metal into gold, believing it would secure her Lord Ravenwood's financial support. She planned to funnel the ill-gotten wealth into James Darkwood's mayoral campaign, ensuring he won the election. Once Darkwood sat in the mayor's chair, Poison Ivy would wield influence over him, and ultimately seize control over Nightshade City. But Eleanor had been an obstacle in her path. Refusing to divulge the alchemical secret, Eleanor stood in the way of Poison Ivy's grand scheme. And she paid the ultimate price for her unwavering integrity.

Finally, the truth emerged, like a beacon in the darkness. Sam had uncovered the mastermind behind Eleanor's murder, the one responsible for orchestrating the macabre dance that led to her untimely demise. With the evidence in hand, he brought the poison ivy to justice and ensured that Eleanor's memory would be honoured.

As Nightshade City rejoiced in the long-awaited resolution, Sam found solace in the knowledge that his relentless pursuit had brought closure to Eleanor's loved ones. The pain and grief would never completely fade, but justice had been served.

Sam Wade, the relentless and tenacious investigator, had honoured his promise to Eleanor. As he stood at her grave, he whispered a final farewell, promising to continue fighting for truth and justice in her memory.

And so, the nightshade city slept a little easier, knowing that no matter the darkness that may lurk, there would always be those like Sam who would rise to unveil the truth, no matter the cost.

The End.

Shadows in the Abbey. A convent Murder Mystery.

Chapter 1: The Serene Sanctuary

In the year 1345, nestled amidst the undulating landscape of rolling hills and verdant meadows stretching as far as the eye could see, there stood a sanctuary of utmost serenity and devotion: St. Agnes Abbey. Nestled amidst nature's embrace, this secluded convent beckoned to noblewomen yearning for solace and a deep connection with the divine.

St. Agnes Abbey was renowned throughout the region for its unwavering commitment to spiritual tranquility. It served as a haven for those noblewomen who sought respite from the chaos and demands of their noble households, a sanctuary where they could immerse themselves in prayer, contemplation, and religious devotion.

The abbey's architectural beauty was a testament to the faith and craftsmanship of its inhabitants. Its elegant stone walls rose majestically, adorned with intricate carvings that depicted scenes from biblical stories and saints' lives. The sun's warm golden rays, filtering through the stained glass windows, painted kaleidoscopic patterns of light upon the abbey's hallowed halls, creating an otherworldly ambiance that seemed to transcend earthly existence.

Within the abbey's walls, the noblewomen lived a life of austere simplicity. Each day, they dedicated themselves to a rigorous routine of prayer, study, and manual labor. The sisters of St. Agnes Abbey found solace in the rhythm of their daily rituals, as they sought to deepen their spiritual connection and grow closer to God.

The abbey's library, a treasure trove of wisdom and knowledge, housed countless manuscripts painstakingly transcribed by the devoted sisters. These revered texts, ranging from sacred scriptures to classical works of philosophy and literature, provided a wellspring of inspiration and intellectual nourishment for the noblewomen. Here, within the hallowed halls, they delved into the profound teachings of theologians, pondered the mysteries of existence, and explored the depths of human thought.

The abbey's chapel, the heart and soul of St. Agnes, resounded with ethereal chants and melodic hymns, as the sisters gathered in harmonious unity to lift their voices in praise and supplication. The air was thick with the fragrance of incense, mingling with the pure voices of the choir, creating an atmosphere of transcendence that transported all who entered to a realm beyond the material world.

Beyond their spiritual pursuits, the noblewomen of St. Agnes Abbey also engaged in works of charity and service to the wider community. They welcomed the destitute, the sick, and the weary, offering them shelter, sustenance, and solace. The abbey's lush gardens and bountiful orchards provided a source of sustenance, enabling the sisters to extend kindness and compassion to those in need.

As the years passed, the reputation of St. Agnes Abbey grew, and noblewomen from far and wide sought entrance to its sacred walls. They were drawn to the abbey's profound sense of spiritual tranquility, the opportunity to cultivate a deep connection with God, and the chance to find solace amidst the chaos of the world.

Chapter 2: A Grisly Discovery

As the first rays of the morning sun brushed the heavens, casting a radiant tapestry of gold and amber across the sky, Sister Mary, a dedicated nun renowned for her tender care of the abbey's herb garden, embarked on her routine pilgrimage to gather the precious ingredients required for the abbey's sacred medicinal tinctures. The herb garden, nestled within the tranquil embrace of the abbey's walls, was a sanctuary of life and healing, where the vibrant aromas of nature mingled with the gentle whispers of the wind.

However, on this fateful morning, the peaceful serenity was shattered by a ghastly sight that sent chills running down Sister Mary's spine. As she ventured further into the herb garden, her heart pounding with trepidation, she stumbled upon an unimaginable horror—the lifeless body of Sister Agatha, a beloved member of the abbey's sisterhood. Sister Agatha's countenance, once radiant and serene, was now frozen in a mask of terror, her eyes wide and her mouth agape in a silent scream.

A wave of shock and sorrow washed over Sister Mary as she knelt beside her fallen sister, her hands trembling with a mixture of grief and disbelief. Sister Agatha had been a pillar of strength within the abbey, her unwavering faith and compassionate nature touching the lives of all who knew her. How could such a gentle soul meet such a tragic end?

Sister Mary's mind raced with questions and apprehension. She knew that the abbey, secluded from the outside world, was a sanctuary of peace, a refuge where the troubles of the world seldom intruded. Yet, within its hallowed walls, a sinister secret had now been unveiled.

With utmost care, Sister Mary rose to her feet and hastened to the abbey, her footsteps echoing through the silent corridors as she sought the counsel of Mother Superior. The gravity of the situation weighed heavily upon her, for the tranquility of the abbey had been shattered, and the safety of the sisterhood was now in jeopardy.

As she reached the Mother Superior's chamber, Sister Mary found the wise and revered leader deep in prayer, her wrinkled hands clasped tightly, seeking solace and guidance from above. Gently, Sister Mary interrupted the sacred silence, recounting the haunting discovery she had made in the herb garden.

Sister Helena's eyes widened with a mixture of grief and concern. She had watched Sister Agatha grow from a timid novice to a beacon of light within the abbey, her devotion and compassion touching the hearts of the community.

News of the tragedy spread swiftly throughout the abbey like an invisible current, sending ripples of shock and sorrow through the hearts of the sisters. Sister Agatha, renowned for her gentle demeanor and her unwavering commitment to the spiritual well-being of her fellow sisters, had been a beloved figure within the community. Her sudden demise struck a deep chord of grief and confusion among those who knew her.

Sister Helena, a woman of profound wisdom and grace, summoned the sisters to the abbey's grand hall. Clad in flowing black robes, the women gathered, their faces etched with sorrow and apprehension. Sister Helena's voice, calm yet tinged with concern, resonated through the somber room, breaking the heavy silence.

"My dear sisters," she began, her gaze sweeping across the sea of expectant faces, "we gather here today to mourn the untimely loss of our dear Sister Agatha. Her presence among us was a beacon of light, and her departure leaves a void that cannot be easily filled."

A collective murmur of agreement rippled through the assembly, underscoring the profound impact Sister Agatha had made on their lives. The weight of her absence hung heavily in the air, leaving the sisters yearning for answers.

"As we mourn our sister, we must also strive to unravel the mystery surrounding her tragic demise," continued Sister Helena, her voice filled with determination. "Let us not succumb to fear or despair, but instead, let us join forces in seeking the truth, for it is our duty to honor Sister Agatha's memory and ensure justice is served."

The sisters nodded, their expressions a blend of grief, resolve, and a shared determination to uncover the truth. They understood that the harmony of their sacred haven had been shattered, and only by lifting the shroud of mystery surrounding Sister Agatha's death could they restore the tranquility that had once enveloped the abbey.

Chapter 3: The Mysterious Demise of Sister Agatha

Sister Helena, the wise and seasoned Mother Superior with deep lines etched upon her face, recognising the urgent need for action, summoned Sister Elizabeth, a young and astute novice known for her sharp wit and insatiable curiosity. Sister Elizabeth's reputation for unraveling perplexing enigmas had reached even the ears of the venerable abbess, who saw in her a glimmer of hope in this dark hour.

In the dimly lit study, where the scent of old parchment lingered, Sister Elizabeth stood before Sister Helena, her eyes filled with a blend of determination and trepidation. The Mother Superior her voice tinged with a mix of sorrow and resolve, spoke with a commanding yet compassionate tone. "Sister Elizabeth, a shadow has fallen upon our abbey, and we must seek the truth behind Sister Agatha's untimely passing. I beseech you to employ your keen intellect and unwavering spirit in this investigation."

Sister Elizabeth nodded solemnly, her mind racing with thoughts of the mystery that lay ahead. She understood the gravity of the task entrusted to her, for the truth held the power to heal the wounds of grief and restore peace to their sacred sanctuary. With a resolute heart, she embarked on her quest for answers, determined to honor the memory of Sister Agatha and bring solace to her grieving sisters.

Chapter 4: Veiled Intrigues

Sister Agatha, had been a woman of boundless compassion and wisdom. Her gentle demeanor and empathetic nature had earned her the trust of her fellow nuns, who confided in her as a confessor and a friend. The novice began her inquiry by visiting each nun in turn, her inquiries gentle yet persistent. She listened intently to their sorrowful stories, searching for fragments of information that might shed light on the events leading to Sister Agatha's demise. One by one, the nuns recounted their last encounters with the departed sister, sharing anecdotes and memories, hoping to contribute to the puzzle that now consumed their lives. Sister Mary Catherine, with her piercing gaze and cryptic smiles, seemed to possess knowledge beyond her years. Her soft-spoken demeanor concealed a cunning intellect, leaving Sister Elizabeth questioning the depths of her involvement. Was she a confidante or a puppet master, pulling strings from the shadows?

Sister Margaret, known for her impeccable attention to detail and unwavering devotion, had always been a pillar of strength within the abbey. Yet, whispers circulated among the sisters, hinting at a clandestine affair that threatened to tarnish her virtuous reputation. Could a heart consumed by forbidden love drive someone to commit murder?

And then there was Sister Marie Claire whose gentle disposition and kind heart were a balm to the troubled souls seeking solace in the abbey's embrace. Yet, recent events had cast a pall over her spirit, and her once luminous eyes now held a flicker of fear. What dark secret haunted her, and how far would she go to protect it?

Chapter 5: The Enigmatic Alchemist

Among the inhabitants of the ancient abbey nestled amidst the rolling hills, there lived a man known as Brother Ambrose. Revered and whispered about in hushed tones, he was a renowned alchemist, his name echoing through the corridors of time. Yet, his fame was intertwined with a veil of eccentricities and an enigmatic demeanor that surrounded him like a shroud.

Sister Elizabeth, a young and astute nun, possessed a keen perception that went beyond the realm of mere mortals. She sensed there was more to the tragic murder of Sister Agatha than met the eye. Her intuition, a flame burning within her, led her to believe that Brother Ambrose held the elusive key to unlocking the truth that lay concealed within the shadows of the abbey's walls.

Driven by a relentless pursuit of justice, Sister Elizabeth resolved to seek the counsel of the alchemist. With each step she took towards his secluded chamber, a mixture of anticipation and trepidation coursed through her veins. The corridors seemed narrower, the air heavier, as if the very walls of the abbey bore witness to her purpose.

Finally, she stood before the door to Brother Ambrose's chamber, a threshold to the unknown. Raising her hand, she knocked, the sound reverberating through the silence of the hallway. It took but a moment, yet it felt like an eternity before the door creaked open with a heavy sigh.

Brother Ambrose, clad in a robe of deep crimson, greeted Sister Elizabeth with a gaze that seemed to penetrate her soul. His eyes, an abstruse reflection of ancient wisdom, held a flicker of recognition as he ushered her inside. The chamber itself was a testament to his enigmatic nature—shelves lined with dusty tomes, glass vials filled with mysterious liquids, and arcane symbols etched upon the walls.

As Sister Elizabeth tentatively broached the topic of Sister Agatha's untimely demise, Brother Ambrose's face betrayed a fleeting expression of sadness, quickly hidden beneath a facade of impenetrability. He spoke in riddles and metaphors, his words dancing on the edge of comprehension.

"Truth, my dear sister, is a delicate flower that blooms amidst the thorns of secrecy," he whispered, his voice a mere whisper carried by the wind. "To find the answers you seek, you must journey beyond the confines of what you consider real."

Intrigued yet frustrated by his cryptic response, Sister Elizabeth pressed further, her eyes locked with his. It was then that she noticed a subtle shift in Brother Ambrose's countenance, a glimmer of vulnerability that flickered like a candle in the dark.

With a sigh that seemed to carry the weight of countless untold stories, he confessed, "I, too, bear my own dark secrets, dear sister. Secrets that haunt me, that I have tried to bury within the depths of my being. But the truth has a way of resurfacing, demanding to be seen."

As the words hung in the air, Sister Elizabeth found herself caught in a whirlwind of emotions the more

she delved deeper into her investigation, the more she discovered subtle nuances and hidden tensions that had previously eluded her. Beneath the veil of mourning, there were whispers of discontent, forbidden love affairs that had blossomed and withered in the shadows, the clandestine rendezvous that defied the vows of chastity and obedience, all this and more unveiled before her searching eyes. The lives of these pious women, dedicated to their faith and devotion, were intertwined in ways she could never have fathomed. fractured relationships, and long-held secrets. It became clear that the tranquil facade of the abbey concealed a complex tapestry of human emotions and tangled bonds, waiting to be unraveled.

Chapter 6: The Love That Defied Conventions

In an intense and gripping conversation, Sister Marie Claire, her heart racing, musters the courage to confide in Sister Elizabeth about the clandestine affair between Sister Margaret and Brother Ambrose. As she pours out her anguish, Marie Claire's words tremble with a mix of betrayal and vulnerability. She recounts the moments of suspicion that gradually unraveled the truth, that one of the two people who new of the affair was dead- murdered, leaving her in fear for her life. Tears well in her eyes as she describes the painful realisation that Sister Margaret or Brother Ambrose maybe a killer.

Sister Margaret and Brother Ambrose were seemingly bound by their shared devotion to their faith. Both had dedicated their lives to serving God and their respective communities. Sister Margaret , a gentle and compassionate nun, found solace in her vows, while Brother Ambrose, an eloquent and respected priest, found purpose in guiding his flock. Little did they know that their paths would converge in a way that would challenge their devotion and reshape their lives forever.

Their first encounter was innocent, a chance meeting in the garden when he first came to the abbey to take confession. They had become engaged in a theological discussions, their intellectual connection quickly blossomed into something more profound. Their conversations were filled with a profound understanding and a shared passion for spirituality. It was as if they were two souls meant to find solace in one another, despite the boundaries that separated them.

But as their friendship deepened, so did their feelings for each other. Sister Margaret and Brother Ambrose found themselves in a whirlwind of conflicting emotions. The love they felt was strong, undeniable, and yet forbidden by the very vows they had taken. They had tried to suppress their feelings, but love is a force that cannot be easily restrained.

Their love affair began secretly, hidden from the prying eyes of their community. In the quiet corners of the convent and the confessional booth, their stolen moments became a refuge from the tumultuous storm of emotions they battled within themselves. They knew the risks they were taking, but the intensity of their love outweighed their fears. Weeks turned into months, and the depth of their love grew alongside their hidden secret. Their clandestine affair had consequences that could not be ignored. Sister Margaret discovered that she was pregnant with Brother Ambrose's child. Their joy was tinged with a profound sense of guilt and fear, for they knew that their child would be a living testament to their forbidden love.

Knowing that their child's existence would forever alter the course of their lives and bring shame upon their respective religious orders, they made the painful decision to keep their secret hidden from the world. With heavy hearts, they had entrusted the truth only to a select few.

One of those few was Sister Marie Claire, a trusted confidante and fellow nun. Sister Agatha, a close friend of Sister Margaret, happened to overhear their conversation about the secret child. Consumed by a mix of curiosity and concern, Sister Agatha approached Sister Marie Claire, desperately seeking answers.

Sister Marie Claire, torn between loyalty and the need to unburden herself, made the decision to share the secret with Sister Agatha. She believed that revealing the truth might bring some solace to her troubled heart and offer a glimmer of hope for the child born out of love.

In a quiet corner of the convent, Sister Margaret, with tears in her eyes, had disclosed the forbidden affair between Sister Margaret and Brother Ambrose and the existence of their child. Sister Agatha had listened intently, her heart heavy with the weight of the secret she now carried.

The revelation had shaken Sister Agatha to her core, challenging the beliefs and convictions she held dear. She was torn between her loyalty to her friends and the knowledge that the truth could shatter the lives they had built. Uncertain of what to do, Sister Agatha had grappled with her conscience, knowing that her decision could forever alter the course of their lives.

Chapter 7: Unveiling the Veil of Deception

In a frantic race against the relentless grip of time, Sister Elizabeth embarked on a perilous journey to unravel the intricate tapestry of lies and deceit that had insidiously woven itself around the sacred walls of the abbey. Determined and resolute, she delved deep into the murky depths of the abbey's secrets, driven by an unwavering commitment to justice.

With unwavering determination and a keen eye for detail, Sister Elizabeth meticulously pieced together the fragments of information that lay strewn about like puzzle pieces. Each revelation brought forth a new thread, weaving together the strands of a complex web of intrigue. The once-veiled truth began to emerge, casting a haunting shadow over the convent's hallowed halls.

Whispers echoed through the halls, and the sisters' gazes turned furtive whenever Sister Elizabeth drew near. They sensed her growing proximity to the heart of the mystery, and fear gnawed at their insides. The murderer, once secure in their anonymity, now found themselves exposed to the relentless pursuit of justice. Sister Elizabeth's resolve remained unyielding. She knew that the path she walked was fraught with danger, that the truth she sought might unleash a storm of chaos within the sacred walls of the abbey. Yet, she also understood that only by unmasking the murderer could order be restored and the wounds of betrayal begin to heal.

With every passing day, the web of intrigue grew tighter, the stakes higher. Sister Elizabeth's trust, already tenuous, was stretched to its limits. She had to tread carefully, for the abbey had become a labyrinth of lies, where even the most innocent gesture could hide a dagger.

As the tendrils of truth took hold, the atmosphere within the abbey grew heavy, burdened by the weight of long-suppressed secrets. Whispers echoed through the corridors, carrying the tremors of uncertainty and fear. Sister Elizabeth, undeterred by the mounting tension, pressed forward, her faith in her pursuit unwavering.

Chapter 8: A Secret Unveiled

As the moon cast a soft, ethereal glow across the tranquil garden, Sister Elizabeth anxiously awaited the arrival of Sister Margaret and Brother Ambrose, she knew this was the one chance she had to force the murderer to act to protect their secret. Sister Margaret's figure emerged from the shadows, her face illuminated by trepidation. Brother Ambrose, always dependable, followed closely behind, his eyes reflecting a silent determination.

Sister Elizabeth greeted them the time had come to reveal the truth that had been hidden for far too long. She led them to a secluded corner of the garden, where the fragrance of jasmine mingled with the gentle rustling of leaves.

Sister Margaret and Brother Ambrose settled onto a stone bench, their eyes searching one another's faces for reassurance. The air crackled with anticipation as Sister Elizabeth took a deep breath, steeling herself for the momentous conversation that lay ahead.

"Sister Margaret, Brother Ambrose," she began, her voice steady but laced with emotion. "I have called you here tonight because it is time for your secret to see the light of day. You can no longer bear the weight of this burden alone."

Sister Margaret, leaned forward. "What is this secret, Sister Elizabeth? You have spoken of it in hushed whispers."

Sister Elizabeth reached out and clasped Sister Margaret's hand, offering silent support. "Your secret, dear sister, concerns your baby. Tomorrow, I have arranged to meet with Sister Helena and reveal the truth."

Brother Ambrose, his brow furrowed, interjected with concern. "Sister Elizabeth, are you certain this is the right course of action? Revealing such a secret could have far-reaching consequences."

Sister Elizabeth nodded, her eyes filled with resolve. "Brother Ambrose, you have carried this secret for far too long. It has weighed heavily on your souls, and it is time to release it. Sister Helena deserves to know the truth, and we must trust in her wisdom and compassion."

Chapter 9: Unveiling Darkness

Sister Elizabeth's heart pounded in her chest as she made her way through the dimly lit corridors of St. Agnes's Abbey. Her steps were cautious, each footfall echoing in the silence that enveloped the building. She knew that time was of the essence; she had to reach Sister Helena's office and put her plan into action before it was too late.

As she approached the door, Sister Elizabeth noticed a faint flickering light seeping through the small glass windowpane. Confusion crept into her mind; why would there be light coming from within? Taking a deep breath, she pushed open the heavy wooden door and stepped inside.

To her surprise, darkness greeted her instead. The room was void of any source of illumination except for a single candle placed on Sister Helena's desk, casting eerie shadows across the walls. Sister Elizabeth paused for a moment, allowing her eyes to adjust to this unexpected change in atmosphere.

Suddenly, a chilling voice broke through the silence. "You shouldn't have come here," whispered Sister Margaret from somewhere within the darkness.

Sister Elizabeth spun around in alarm, searching for its source. "Sister Margaret? What are you doing here? Where is Sister Helena?"

The sound of footsteps echoed closer until Sister Margaret emerged from behind an old bookshelf near the window. Her eyes glimmered with malice as she looked upon Sister Elizabeth with wild abandon.

"Sister Agatha deserved what happened to her," Sister Margaret hissed venomously, taking slow and deliberate steps toward her fellow nun.

Sister Elizabeth took an instinctive step back, feeling fear within her being. "What are you saying? You know something about Sister Agatha's death?"

A twisted smile played at the corners of Sister Margaret's lips as she lunged forward without warning, attempting to catch Sister Elizabeth off guard and overpower her. But years of discipline and inner strength helped Sister Elizabeth react swiftly, sidestepping the attack and pushing Sister Margaret away.

The room seemed to shrink as the two nuns engaged in a desperate struggle. The flickering candlelight cast their shadows upon the walls, mirroring their tangled movements. Each gasp for breath was accompanied by grunts of determination and fear.

As they wrestled, Sister Margaret's eyes locked with Sister Elizabeth's. Her face contorted with anguish and guilt as she fought against her fellow sister's unwavering resolve. In that moment, something within Sister Margaret broke, and words spilled forth uncontrollably.

"I killed her," she admitted through gritted teeth, tears streaming down her face. "I couldn't stand her righteousness anymore. She saw through my façade."

Sister Elizabeth froze, disbelief washing over her like a tidal wave. She never anticipated such a confession from someone who had seemingly devoted herself to a life of service and piety.

"Why?" Sister Elizabeth managed to whisper, struggling to comprehend the magnitude of what she had just heard.

Sister Margaret's voice wavered with self-loathing as she continued to fight against both her physical confinement and inner demons. "She knew about...about my past sins," she confessed shakily. "She threatened to expose."

Tears welled up in Sister Elizabeth's eyes as she realized the complexity of this situation – not only had there been a murder committed within these sacred walls but also an intricate web of secrets woven among them all.

Just then, footsteps echoed outside the office door followed by Sister Helena's voice. The struggle ceased momentarily as both nuns turned their attention toward this unexpected interruption.

With one final push against Sister Margaret's faltering resistance, Sister Elizabeth managed to break free from their entangled embrace. She stumbled backward towards the door just as Sister Helena entered the office, her face a mix of concern and confusion.

Sister Elizabeth's voice trembled as she pointed to Sister Margaret. "Sister Helena she confessed...she admitted to murdering Sister Agatha."

The room fell silent once more, the weight of Sister Margaret's confession hanging heavily in the air. Sister Helena's eyes widened with shock before quickly regaining her composure.Sister Margaret, is there any truth to these accusations?" Sister Helena asked gently but firmly.

Sister Margaret's face paled visibly, beads of sweat forming on her forehead. She opened her mouth to speak but found herself at a loss for words.

"I...I..." she stammered, searching desperately for an explanation that could absolve her from this grave accusation.

But no plausible defense emerged from her trembling lips—her guilt had been laid bare. The cold grip of realisation settled upon those present; they were witnessing the unmasking of a murderer within their midst.

As the gravity of the situation took hold, sorrow mingled with shock.Sister Helena mourned not only for Sister Agatha's tragic passing but also for the betrayal she felt at discovering one of her own was responsible for such a heinous act.

Through tear-filled eyes, Sister Helena addressed Sister Margaret one final time:

"Sister Margaret, it is clear that you have committed a grievous sin against both God and your fellow sister Agatha," she said solemnly. "I shall contact the sheriff immediately so that justice may be served."

"Thank you, Sister Elizabeth," Sister Helena said gravely. "I must bring this matter to light and seek justice for our fallen sister."

The revelation sent shockwaves through the sisterhood, their faith in their fellow sisters shattered by the revelation that evil had walked among them. Justice had prevailed, but not without leaving scars etched in the hearts of those who had witnessed the tragedy.

As the sun bathed the abbey in its warm, forgiving light, the sisters grappled with the aftermath of the harrowing ordeal. From this day forward, trust would be harder to come by as they grappled with the unsettling truth that darkness could reside even where there was supposed to be light.

The abbey, forever changed, began the process of healing, stitching together the fragments of a fractured sisterhood. With the passage of time, the wounds began to heal, and the abbey emerged from the shadows, stronger and more united than ever before. The echoes of the past remained, serving as a reminder of the fragility of trust and the unwavering commitment required to safeguard the sanctity of their sacred haven.

The Murder of Reginald Harrington. A Holmes, Watson and Christie Murder Mystery.

Chapter 1: The Strange Fog

It was a cool and misty evening in London when Sherlock Holmes and his loyal companion, Dr. John Watson, decided to take a leisurely stroll along the Thames. Little did they know that their ordinary evening walk would lead them into a most extraordinary adventure. They often found solace in these walks, discussing complex cases and exchanging opinions on various detective novels. As they ventured deeper into the evening, an eerie fog blanketed the city, obscuring their surroundings. The fog, dense and mysterious, seemed to have a life of its own. Holmes curiously peered through the haze, the detective in him awakened by the unusual phenomenon.

"Watson, do you notice anything peculiar about this fog?" Holmes inquired, his sharp eyes scanning the surroundings. Watson squinted, attempting to discern something extraordinary amidst the opacity. "I can't say that I do, Holmes. It's just a typical fog that occasionally engulfs London."

Holmes, ever the skeptic, wasn't convinced by Watson's casual response. "This fog is different, Watson. It feels... almost alive," he mused, his mind already whirling with countless deductions.

As they continued their walk, the fog seemed to grow thicker and more suffocating. The gas lamps lining the streets emitted feeble, flickering light, casting eerie shadows that danced with the mist. Holmes and Watson pressed on, their senses heightened by the unusual atmosphere. Suddenly, a chilling gust of wind swept through the fog, causing Holmes to shiver involuntarily. He stopped in his tracks, his eyes narrowing as he analyzed the surroundings. "Watson, there is something amiss here," he declared, his voice filled with a mix of curiosity and concern.

Watson, ever the loyal companion, stood beside Holmes, his gaze mirroring the detective's intensity. "What do you think it could be, Holmes?" he asked, his voice steady despite the growing unease in the air.

Holmes took a moment to observe the fog, his mind working at lightning speed. "It's as if the fog is hiding something, Watson. Something that doesn't want to be discovered," he replied, his voice filled with a sense of urgency.

As they ventured further into the fog, Holmes and Watson noticed strange figures moving in the distance. Shadows darted and shifted, their forms distorted by the mist. Holmes pulled out his magnifying glass and examined the figures with precision. "These are not ordinary shadows, Watson. They have a purpose, a direction," he murmured, his eyes never leaving the mysterious figures.

Watson's heart raced with anticipation as he followed Holmes' lead. The fog seemed to whisper secrets, enticing them to uncover its hidden truths. They followed the figures through narrow alleyways and winding streets, their determination unwavering. Little did they know, this strange fog was just the beginning of an adventure that would test their skills and challenge their beliefs.

Chapter 2: A Time Traveling Journey

When the fog finally lifted, Holmes and Watson found themselves in the year 1920, standing in a quaint English village. The atmosphere felt different, and the architecture had a distinctively vintage charm. They soon discovered that they had been transported to the era of the renowned crime writer, Agatha Christie. As they tried to make sense of their situation, a commotion caught their attention. A crowd had gathered around a grand estate, whispering about a murder that had taken place. Intrigued by the prospect of a real-life mystery, Holmes and Watson made their way through the crowd, their detective instincts kicking into high gear.

As they approached the estate, Holmes and Watson noticed the police cordoning off the area, ensuring that no one tampered with the crime scene. The victim, a wealthy aristocrat named Lord Harrington, was found dead in his study, a dagger lodged in his chest. The crowd speculated about the possible motives and suspects, but it was clear that the local police were struggling to crack the case.

Unable to resist the allure of a challenging puzzle, Holmes decided to offer his assistance to the local authorities. With his keen observation skills and deductive reasoning, he believed he could unravel the truth behind Lord Harrington's murder. Watson, always eager to assist his friend, followed closely behind.

As they entered the estate, they were greeted by Inspector Williams, who was initially skeptical of Holmes' involvement. However, after witnessing Holmes' remarkable deductions in a few minor details of the crime scene, Williams agreed to let him assist in the investigation.

Chapter 3: The Meeting with Agatha Christie

Inside the estate, they saw a woman, her presence commanding and elegant, holding a book firmly in her hands. She introduced herself as Agatha Christie, England's celebrated crime novelist. Agatha, much to their surprise, revealed that she was currently working on a new novel but had unexpectedly found herself embroiled in a real-life murder mystery. Astounded by the meeting, Holmes and Watson composed themselves and explained the sequence of events that led them here. Agatha Christie herself, equally fascinated by the sudden appearance of the legendary detective and his companion, welcomed their assistance in unraveling the enigma that had befallen the village.

Agatha led Holmes and Watson to a cozy study, adorned with bookshelves filled with her own works as well as various crime novels from around the world. The room exuded an air of mystery, with dim lighting and the faint scent of old books.

As they settled in, Agatha began to recount the events that had unfolded in the village. A wealthy businessman, Sir Charles Harrington, had been found dead in his study under suspicious circumstances. The local police had been unable to make any progress in the investigation, and the villagers were growing increasingly fearful.

Holmes listened intently, occasionally interjecting with questions to clarify certain details. Agatha's storytelling skills were evident as she painted a vivid picture of the village and its inhabitants, each with their own secrets and motives.

With her permission, Holmes and Watson examined the crime scene. They meticulously inspected every inch of the study, taking note of the placement of the furniture, the position of the body, and any other potential clues. Holmes's keen eye and deductive reasoning allowed him to uncover subtle details that others might have missed.

Back in the study, Holmes and Watson discussed their findings with Agatha. They shared their theories and speculated on possible suspects, motives, and alibis. Agatha's own insights proved invaluable, as she provided a unique perspective as both a writer and a keen observer of human behavior.

As Holmes and Watson delved deeper into the mystery, they interviewed the villagers, searching for any inconsistencies or hidden truths. Agatha, always by their side, offered guidance and encouragement, her presence a constant reminder of the importance of storytelling and attention to detail.

Chapter 4: The Murdered Millionaire

The victim was Sir Reginald Harrington, a wealthy and influential member of the community. His body was found in the study. The circumstances were mysterious, and the evidence was perplexing. Holmes and Watson carefully examined the crime scene, meticulously analyzing every detail. The autopsy report stated that he had been bludgeoned to death with a blunt instrument, possibly a candlestick. There was no sign of forced entry, leading them to believe that the perpetrator was someone familiar with the house. No one was beyond suspicion; the suspects included Sir Reginald's estranged family members, jealous business associates, and even the loyal household staff. Each had their own reasons to desire Sir Reginald's demise. As Holmes and Watson delved deeper into the investigation, they discovered a web of secrets and hidden motives within Sir Reginald's life. They began by interviewing the estranged family members, starting with his wife, Lady Genevieve Harrington. She was known for her extravagant lifestyle and had been living separately from Sir Reginald for quite some time. Lady Genevieve claimed to have an alibi, as she was attending a charity event on the night of the murder.

Next on the list was Sir Reginald's son, Charles Harrington, who had a strained relationship with his father due to their conflicting interests. Charles had been trying to convince his father to invest in a risky business venture, but Sir Reginald had adamantly refused. The tension between them was palpable, and Charles had a clear motive for wanting his father out of the way.

Another suspect was Sir Reginald's brother, Lord Percival Harrington, who had always been envious of his brother's success and wealth. Lord Percival had been struggling financially and saw Sir Reginald's demise as an opportunity to inherit his fortune. However, he claimed to have been out of town on business during the time of the murder.

Holmes and Watson also turned their attention to Sir Reginald's business associates, who had a lot to gain from his death. Many of them had been involved in shady dealings and had clashed with Sir Reginald over business decisions. One such associate was Mr. Jonathan Blackwood, who had been vying for a promotion within the company. He had recently been passed over in favor of Sir Reginald's choice, which fueled his resentment and desire for revenge.

The loyal household staff also fell under suspicion, as they had intimate knowledge of the house and its inhabitants. The butler, Mr. Edmundson, had been working for the Harrington family for years and had access to the study where the murder took place. The housemaid, Miss Emily Thompson, had recently been reprimanded by Sir Reginald for her careless behavior, leading to a potential motive for revenge.

Chapter 5: Uncovering Secrets

As they delved deeper into the mystery, following a labyrinth of clues, false leads, and half-truths, Watson stumbled upon a crucial clue. He found a hidden compartment in the study, within which lay a diary. Entries hinted towards an illicit affair between Reginald and a housemaid, and the subsequent shame he felt following the birth of their child. A child whom he had disowned, having dismissed the child's mother, turning her out onto the streets, destitute and alone. Intrigued by this revelation, Watson shared his discovery with Holmes, who immediately recognized the significance of the hidden diary. The entries shed light on Reginald's character and provided a motive for his sudden disappearance.

Holmes and Watson decided to investigate further, seeking out anyone who might have known the housemaid or had information about the child. Their inquiries led them to a nearby village, where they discovered an elderly woman who had once worked as a maid in the same household.

The woman, Mrs. Jenkins, was hesitant to speak at first, fearing retribution from the powerful family. However, Holmes' persuasive skills and genuine concern for the truth eventually won her over. She revealed that the housemaid's name was Emily, and she had indeed given birth to Reginald's child.

According to Mrs. Jenkins, Emily had been a kind and hardworking woman, who had fallen in love with Reginald despite their class differences. When she became pregnant, Emily had hoped that Reginald would marry her and provide a better life for their child. However, Reginald's pride and the pressure from his family had led him to abandon both Emily and their baby.

Chapter 6: The Search for Truth

This provided a new direction to their investigation. Driven by a sense of justice, Holmes and Watson tracked down Emily, who had been living in poverty and despair ever since Reginald had cast her aside. They found her in a rundown tenement, barely surviving on odd jobs and charity. The once vibrant and hopeful woman was now a shadow of her former self. Upon questioning, she admitted to the affair but vehemently denied any hand in Reginald's death. As for the child, he had been put up for adoption twenty years ago when he was 5 years old. Moved by her plight, Holmes and Watson vowed to help Emily. They used their connections to secure a small but comfortable home for her and arranged for financial support to ensure she could provide for her needs. Emily was overwhelmed with gratitude, finally finding some solace after years of suffering.

Meanwhile, Holmes continued to dig deeper into Reginald's disappearance, suspecting that his actions towards Emily and their child might have triggered a sequence of events leading to his murder.

Chapter 7: The Mysterious Acquaintance

Sherlock, Watson, and Agatha reviewed the diary again and noticed a pattern. Reginald's guilt and paranoia escalated every time he wrote about meeting a mysterious acquaintance. This acquaintance, only referred to as 'F', was not mentioned in earlier entries. They decided to identify this 'F' and soon found a likely candidate, Mr. Frederick Barnard, a recent acquaintance of Reginald Harrington. Mr. Frederick Barnard was an enigmatic figure known for his elusive nature and involvement in various secretive activities. Sherlock, Watson, and Agatha delved into their investigation, determined to uncover the truth behind this mysterious acquaintance and his connection to Reginald's escalating guilt.

They began by gathering information about Mr. Barnard's background. They discovered that he had a reputation for being involved in underground dealings and had a network of connections with individuals involved in shady businesses. His name had come up in previous investigations, but he had always managed to elude capture.

To get closer to the truth, Sherlock devised a plan to approach Mr. Barnard under the guise of seeking his assistance with another case. They set up a meeting in a discreet location, a dimly lit café known for its secrecy.

As they waited for Mr. Barnard to arrive, Sherlock carefully observed the surroundings, noting the nervous glances exchanged between the café's patrons. It was clear that this place attracted individuals with secrets to hide.

Finally, Mr. Barnard arrived, his tall and slender figure blending seamlessly into the shadows. Sherlock, Watson, and Agatha introduced themselves, explaining their interest in Reginald Harrington's diary and their desire to understand the nature of his relationship with Mr. Barnard.

Mr. Barnard, initially guarded, seemed intrigued by their knowledge of the diary. He agreed to share his side of the story, cautioning them that it might not be what they expected.

Over a cup of steaming coffee, Mr. Barnard began to unravel the truth. He revealed that he had indeed met Reginald Harrington several times, but their encounters were not what they seemed. Contrary to Reginald's perceptions, Mr. Barnard had not been pressuring him or manipulating him into illegal activities.

Instead, Mr. Barnard had been concerned about Reginald's well-being. He had recognized the signs of Reginald's growing guilt and paranoia and had tried to offer support and guidance. Mr. Barnard had been aware of Reginald's involvement in a secret society, one that Reginald had joined with good intentions but had since become disillusioned with.

As Mr. Barnard continued to speak, it became clear that he had been trying to help Reginald escape the clutches of this secret society. He had wanted to protect Reginald from the consequences of his association with them and had been urging him to sever ties and start anew.

Sherlock listened intently, piecing together the puzzle. He realized that Reginald's guilt and paranoia were not entirely unfounded. The secret society had been involved in criminal activities, and Reginald had become an unwitting accomplice.

With this new understanding, Sherlock, Watson, and Agatha thanked Mr. Barnard for his honesty and assistance. They now had a clearer picture of the events that had led to Reginald's demise.

Chapter 8: Unraveling the Truth

As Sherlock delves deeper into the investigation, he discovers subtle yet telling signs that hint at an unspoken connection between Frederick and the deceased, Sir Reginald Harrington. Additionally, an old family portrait that Sherlock uncovers shows a remarkable resemblance between Frederick and Sir Reginald. Determined to confirm his suspicions, Holmes dug into Frederick's past, finding adoption records that revealed a startling fact - Frederick Barnard was indeed the adopted son of Sir Reginald Harrington. With this newfound knowledge, Sherlock's mind raced with possibilities. The dynamic trio decided to focus their attention on the adopted child. They tirelessly searched through adoption records and tracked down the agency responsible for the adoption twenty years ago. With their renowned powers of deduction, they managed to uncover the child's current whereabouts.

Sherlock, Agatha, and Watson wasted no time in seeking out the adopted child, hoping that he held the key to solving the mystery. They found him living a quiet life in a small town, completely unaware of his true parentage. Intrigued by their unexpected visit, he welcomed them into his home.

During their conversation, the adopted child revealed that he had always felt a sense of emptiness and a longing to discover his true roots. He had recently embarked on a personal journey to uncover his biological family's history.

Chapter 9: Unveiling the Hidden Room: Secrets and Betrayals

As Holmes and Watson continued to gather evidence, they discovered a hidden secret room in Sir Reginald's study. Inside, they found a collection of incriminating documents and letters that hinted at blackmail and illegal activities. It seemed that Sir Reginald had been involved in a web of deceit that had caught up with him. These documents revealed a secret business deal that Sir Reginald had been involved in, one that could ruin the reputation of several prominent individuals. With this new information, Holmes and Watson began to piece together the puzzle. They realized that the murder was not a crime of passion or revenge but rather a carefully planned execution to silence Sir Reginald and protect the secrets he held.

As the investigation reached its climax, Holmes and Watson called for a gathering of all the suspects in the study. With all eyes on them, they dramatically revealed the culprit. The murderer turned out to be none other than Mr. Jonathan Blackwood, the disgruntled business associate. He had discovered Sir Reginald's secret deal and saw it as an opportunity to eliminate him and cover his own tracks.

With the evidence against him overwhelming, Mr. Blackwood confessed to the crime. He admitted to using a candlestick from the study as the murder weapon and staging the scene to make it appear as if someone familiar with the house had committed the crime. His motive was revenge and self-preservation, as he believed that Sir Reginald's secret would ruin his own reputation and career.

Chapter 10: Farewell to Agatha Christie

The mysterious fog returned, and Holmes and Watson bid farewell to Agatha Christie, grateful for the unique adventure they had shared. They returned to their own time, carrying with them the memories of their extraordinary encounter. From that day forward, Holmes and Watson cherished their friendship with Agatha Christie, knowing that their paths had crossed in a most extraordinary way. Though they returned to their usual investigations, they would forever treasure the time they spent in 1920, solving a real-life murder alongside one of the greatest mystery writers of all time.

Chapter 11: The Legacy Lives On

Back in their own time, Holmes and Watson couldn't help but reflect on the incredible journey they had experienced. The memory of their collaboration with Agatha Christie lingered in their minds, reminding them of the power of teamwork and the thrill of solving a perplexing mystery.

Inspired by their encounter, Holmes and Watson continued to hone their detective skills, taking on increasingly complex cases. They found themselves applying Agatha's storytelling techniques to their investigations, carefully constructing narratives and piecing together clues to uncover the truth.

Their reputation as brilliant detectives grew, and they became known for their uncanny ability to solve the most baffling cases. The legacy of their collaboration with Agatha Christie lived on, inspiring future generations of detectives and mystery writers.

Years later, Holmes and Watson would look back on their time-traveling adventure with fondness and gratitude. The strange fog that had transported them to another era had not only led them to a captivating murder mystery but had also forged a bond with one of the greatest literary minds of their time.

As they continued their work, Holmes and Watson would often find themselves reflecting on the lessons they had learned from Agatha Christie. Her keen insights into human nature and her ability to craft intricate plots served as a constant reminder of the importance of observation, deduction, and perseverance in their own detective work.

Hercules Final Case.

Chapter 1

Hercule Poirot had been feeling unwell for the past month, and he could not shake the feeling that something was not right. He had been experiencing frequent headaches, bouts of dizziness, and persistent fatigue. After consulting with his trusted physician, Dr. Constantine, Poirot had scheduled a follow-up appointment to discuss his symptoms.

As he entered Dr. Constantine's office, Poirot was greeted by a warm smile and a firm handshake. The doctor had known Poirot for many years, and the two men had developed a close relationship based on mutual trust and respect.

"Good morning, Hercule," said Dr. Constantine. "Please, have a seat. How have you been feeling?"

Poirot sighed heavily and leaned back in his chair. "Not well, my friend," he said. "I have been experiencing headaches, dizziness, and fatigue for the past four weeks. I have tried resting, but the symptoms do not seem to go away. I am concerned that something serious may be wrong."

Dr. Constantine nodded sympathetically. "I understand how you feel, Hercule. These symptoms could be indicative of a number of different conditions. I would like to perform a thorough examination and some tests to help us determine the root cause of your discomfort."

Over the course of the next hour, Dr. Constantine conducted a battery of tests on Poirot, including blood work, imaging scans, and a series of neurological evaluations. Despite his initial apprehension, Poirot remained calm and cooperative throughout the process, trusting in the doctor's expertise and judgment.

After completing the tests, Dr. Constantine invited Poirot to sit down once again. "Hercule, I have some news," he said gravely. "Your test results indicate that you have a brain tumor."

Poirot's heart sank. He had suspected that something serious was wrong, but he had never imagined that it would be this dire. "A tumor?" he repeated, his voice barely above a whisper.

Dr. Constantine nodded solemnly. "Yes, Hercule. I'm afraid that the symptoms you have been experiencing are all consistent with a tumor in the brain. We can discuss your treatment options in detail, but we need to act quickly if we are to have any chance of saving your life."

Poirot sat in stunned silence, his mind reeling with the implications of the doctor's words. He had always prided himself on his mental acuity and his ability to solve even the most complex of mysteries, but now he was faced with a challenge that even he could not overcome.

As he left Dr. Constantine's office and made his way back to his apartment, Poirot felt a profound sense of sadness and despair. He knew that his time was limited, and that he would have to make the most of the days he had left. But even in the face of such adversity, he remained resolute and determined, determined to face his fate with courage and grace.

Chapter 2:

Miss Marple received a letter from her old friend, Poirot. He was in dire need of her services. An old acquaintance of his had recently died under suspicious circumstances and he needed her help to investigate it. Miss Marple agreed to travel to Poirot's home to discuss the matter.

Meanwhile, in London, Hastings sat in his study reading the newspaper when he received a call from Poirot. He too was needed to help investigate the death of Poirot's friend. Hastings agreed to meet Poirot at his home.

Hercule Poirot stood in his elaborately decorated sitting room, staring at a small photograph on his desk. The photo depicted a group of people, all in their prime, laughing and enjoying each other's company. Among them was a man Poirot knew quite well, an old friend by the name of Alexander Cavendish. Poirot had just received the news of Alexander's untimely death and he was devastated. But that was not the only reason he had called his dear friends, Miss Marple and Captain Hastings, to his home that day.

As they sat down, Poirot took a deep breath and began to speak. "It appears that I too am faced with mortality, my dear friends. I have been diagnosed with a brain tumor."

Miss Marple and Captain Hastings were both shocked and upset. Poirot was the closest thing they had to family and the thought of losing him was unbearable. But before they could react, Poirot continued.

"I have been told that I have a limited amount of time left, perhaps only a few months. However, there is one last thing I must do before I go. Alexander Cavendish, my old friend, was found dead last night under suspicious circumstances. I believe foul play is involved, but I cannot investigate it myself. That is where you come in."

Despite their own grief, Miss Marple and Captain Hastings agreed to help their friend. They had been through many adventures with Poirot and knew that they could not deny him his last request.

Chapter 3:

Together, the three began to investigate Alexander's death. Poirot, despite his illness, still had the keen mind and sharp wit that he was famous for. Miss Marple and Captain Hastings used their own unique skills to gather information and put the pieces together.

Alexander Cavendish had been found dead in his home, apparently from natural causes. However Poirot suspected foul play as his friend had died suddenly.

Their investigation took them to Alexander's home, where they met his wife, his son, and his daughter-in-law. They also met Alexander's business partner, a man named Edward Carrington. Hastings found Carrington to be an odd character, with shifty eyes and a nervous demeanor.

Alexander's wife, Arabella, was a cold and distant woman. She seemed unaffected by her husband's death, which struck them all as strange. Alexander's son, Jack, and his daughter-in-law, Christine were more forthcoming, it seemed that Alexander had been in contact with a distant relative, a George Barton, who had visited him on a number of occasions prior to his death.

Chapter 4:

Hastings had received a letter from Edward Carrington, who claimed to have information about Alexander's distant relative George Barton. He had been unable to find any substantial information about George Barton, but this letter provided hope.

Hastings decided to pay a visit to Edward Carrington's house, hoping to learn more about George Barton and his connection to Alexander. As he entered the house, he was greeted by a butler who led him to a cozy sitting room where Edward was waiting for him.

"Mr. Hastings, welcome! Please have a seat," Edward said, gesturing towards a comfortable armchair.

"Thank you, Mr. Carrington," Hastings replied, taking a seat. "I appreciate you taking the time to meet with me. I'm quite curious about this George Barton that you mentioned in your letter."

"Of course, Mr. Hastings. Before his death Alexander was doing some research on his family tree and came across George Barton's name. It turns out that he was a distant relative of his,and I have some information about him that might interest you."

Hastings leaned in, eager to hear more. Edward paused for a moment, gathering his thoughts.

"George Barton seemed to have a dubious past, convicted in his youth for petty crimes, he was actually a cousin of Alexander's , but it seems they never had much contact."

Hastings took careful notes as Edward continued. He was pleased to finally have some concrete information about George Barton.

"In fact, I have a letter here that George Barton wrote to Alexander," Edward said, handing a piece of paper to Hastings. "It might shed more light on his relationship with Alexander."

Hastings carefully unfolded the letter and read it over. It was written in a neat, looping script and detailed George's thoughts on Alexander's legacy and George's inheritance.

"This is incredible," Hastings said, looking up at Edward. "Thank you so much for sharing this with me. It gives me a new avenue to explore in my research."

"I'm glad I could be of help," Edward replied with a smile. "If you ever need anything else, don't hesitate to ask."

Hastings thanked Edward and made his way out of the house, feeling energized and eager to continue his research. He had a newfound focus on George Barton, and he was determined to learn everything he could about this long-lost relative of Alexander.

Chapter 5:

Poirot and Hastings decided to try and track down Barton, but their efforts were met with dead ends. No one seemed to know him, nor did anyone recall seeing him around town. Poirot suspected that something was not right and decided to dig deeper.

Finally, after several days of searching, Poirot and Hastings learned that George Barton had been staying at a local hotel.

Hercule Poirot and Captain Hastings arrived at the Empire Hotel, where George Barton had been staying. The hotel staff had informed the manager that Barton had sneaked out of the hotel during the night and had taken his luggage, his hotel bill was still outstanding.

Poirot and Hastings decided to begin their investigation by questioning the hotel staff. They called for the staff to be brought to the lobby for questioning.

First up to be questioned was the hotel receptionist. "Good afternoon, mademoiselle. Can you tell me what you know about George Barton?" Poirot asked, peering at her through his thick-rimmed glasses.

The receptionist, a young woman with curly brown hair, replied, "Well, Monsieur Barton arrived at the hotel four days ago. He was friendly enough, but he kept to himself most of the time. He didn't seem to have any visitors or friends staying with him."

"Did he mention where he was from?" Hastings asked.

"He had a north country accent, sir," the receptionist replied. "But he didn't mention exactly where he was from."

"Did he seem agitated or worried the last time you spoke to him?" Poirot inquired.

"No, sir, he seemed perfectly calm and collected."

Next to be questioned was the hotel porter. "What can you tell me about Mr. Barton?" Poirot asked.

The porter, a middle-aged man with a weathered face, answered, "He was a quiet fellow, sir. Never caused any trouble. He would come and go from the hotel at odd hours. I don't know where he went."

"Did he have any visitors during his stay?" Hastings asked.

"No, sir, at least not that I saw," the porter replied.

Poirot then interviewed the hotel housekeeper. "What can you tell me about Mr. Barton?" he asked.

The housekeeper, a plump woman with a kindly face, replied, "He kept his room very neat and tidy, sir. He didn't have much luggage, just a small valise. I never saw any visitors or heard any noise coming from his room."

"Did he have any phone calls or messages?" Hastings inquired.

"No, sir, not that I'm aware of," the housekeeper said.

Poirot and Hastings thanked the hotel staff for their time and asked the hotel manager if they could see Barton's room.

The hotel staff led Poirot and Hastings to Barton's room. As they entered, they noted that the room was very tidy and organized. Poirot immediately began to observe the various items in the room.

He knew that every clue, no matter how small, could be important in solving the case.

It didn't take long for Poirot to find what he was looking for - a single sheet of paper hidden away in a drawer. Poirot carefully unfolded the letter and began to read it aloud to Hastings.

"My dear Alexander ," Poirot read. "I can't keep this secret to myself any longer. I know what you did to the Smyth family, and I will not hesitate to reveal everything to the world unless you pay me what I am due."

Poirot paused, looking up at Hastings. "It seems, mon ami, that our friend George was involved in some kind of blackmail against Alexander ."

Hastings looked shocked. "Blackmail? But what did he have on Alexander ?"

"That is the question, mon ami," Poirot replied. "But it is clear that George was attempting to extract payment from Alexander in exchange for keeping a scandalous family secret under wraps."

Alexander had refused to pay up, which had led to the deterioration of his health. However, the letter did not reveal what the secret was. Poirot carefully placed the note back where he had found it, taking care not to disturb any other clues, with every clue that he uncovered, Poirot was one step closer to unravelling the mystery of Alexander's death.

Chapter 6:

Miss Marple entered the office of Alexander Cavendish's solicitor, Mr. Robertson, with a sense of unease. She knew that Poroit's dear friend had died under mysterious circumstances, and she hoped that Mr. Robertson could shed some light on the matter.

"Good morning, Miss Marple," Mr. Robertson greeted her with a warm smile. "What brings you here today?"

"I would like to inquire about Mr. Cavendish's Will," replied Miss Marple. "I understand that you were his solicitor."

"Yes, indeed," said Mr. Robertson, his expression turning serious. "Mr. Cavendish was a valued client of mine, and his death was a great loss. May I ask why you are interested in his Will?"

"I have reason to believe that he may have changed it shortly before his death," said Miss Marple. "And I have also heard that the new Will favors Mr. George Barton, who was not in good terms with Mr Cavendish."

Mr. Robertson raised an eyebrow. "That is indeed interesting. I can confirm that Mr. Cavendish did change his Will just a week before his death. And you are correct that the new Will does name Mr. Barton as the primary beneficiary."

"The new Will has raised some suspicions among Mr. Cavendish's friends," said Miss Marple. "They believe that Mr. Barton may have had a hand in its creation."

Mr. Robertson looked thoughtful. "I cannot say for sure, but it is certainly possible. Mr. Barton was present when the new Will was signed, and he did appear to exert some influence over Mr. Cavendish".

"Please continue said Miss Marple "what happened that day".

"As I recall" said Mr Robertson "Alexander Cavendish and George Barton had come to my office with the intention of changing Alexander's Will in favor of George. It was a routine matter, those types of requests are not uncommon, but there was something about the meeting that nagged at me, something that made me uneasy.

I felt George Barton was a man of questionable character. He had recently come into Alexander's life, and I couldn't help but feel that he had an undue influence over Alexander".

"During the meeting, George had done most of the talking. He had been very forceful in his arguments and had a way of convincing Alexander that his way was the right way. I had tried to interject a few times, but George had dismissed my objections as mere technicalities".

"As we went over the details of the Will, I noticed that Alexander seemed hesitant, almost as if he were being coerced into making the changes. I knew that legally, George could not be named as the sole beneficiary of the Will, but I couldn't shake the feeling that something was not right."

"Over the next few days, I spoke to Alexander on the phone several times, trying to gauge his feelings about the Will, but Alexander had been evasive".

Miss Marple nodded. "Thank you for your honesty, Mr. Robertson. I believe this information will be very helpful in my investigation."

"You are welcome, Miss Marple," said Mr. Robertson, his manner respectful. "If you need any further assistance, do not hesitate to ask."

With that, Miss Marple took her leave, her mind racing with new possibilities. She was determined to get to the bottom of this mystery, no matter what it took.

Chapter 7:

Miss Marple sat in Poirot's cosy living room, deep in thought. She had just returned from an informative meeting with Alexander Cavendish's solicitor, Mr. Robertson. She was trying to piece together the mystery surrounding his death and the curious involvement of George Barton. She spent a few moments thinking about what she had learned and what it meant.

As she refocused her mind, she heard the front door open revealing her dear friends, Hercule Poirot and Captain Arthur Hastings.

"Poirot! Hastings! How lovely to see you!" said Miss Marple.

"Miss Marple, it is always a pleasure," said Poirot, kissing the elderly lady's hand. "What brings you such a furrowed brow this evening?"

"I have been unraveling the mystery surrounding Alexander Cavendish's Will," replied Miss Marple, as they entered the sitting room. "I spoke with his solicitor today and discovered that the Will had been changed shortly before Mr. Cavendish's death in favour of George Barton."

Poirot and Hastings exchanged a glance. "That is most concerning," said Poirot. "We have also been investigating Mr. Barton and have found that he had been blackmailing Mr. Cavendish."

"Blackmailing?" repeated Miss Marple, her eyes widening. "Whatever do you mean?"

Hastings took over "Yes, Miss Marple. It appears that Mr. Barton had some damaging information about Mr. Cavendish's past and was using it as leverage to gain control of his finances. Mr. Cavendish was in a difficult position and didn't know what to do. He was very worried about his reputation being tarnished."

Miss Marple frowned. "That does sound very troubling," she said.

"The question now is, did Mr. Barton play a role in Mr. Cavendish's death?" said Poirot, leaning forward.

"We don't have any concrete evidence yet, but the fact that he benefited from the new will certainly makes it appear suspicious," said Miss Marple.

The three of them sat in silence for a moment, pondering the possibilities. Miss Marple was determined to find the truth, no matter how elusive it might be.

Chapter 8:

Hercule Poirot arrived at the home of Alexander Cavendish's family. He had all the information he needed except for one piece and he had come to persuade Arabella to allow an autopsy to be performed.

As he was ushered into the sitting room, Poirot was greeted by the somber faces of Alexander's family. "Mr. Poirot, thank you for coming," said Arabella, Alexander's wife" This is a difficult time for us."

"I understand completely. Please allow me to offer my sincerest condolences for your loss," said Poirot, bowing slightly.

"Thank you. It is a great shock to lose a husband so suddenly," Arabella said "We don't understand what happened."

"That is why I am here, Mrs Cavandish I would like to request that an autopsy be performed on Alexander's body to determine the cause of death," said Poirot, taking a seat opposite the family.

"I don't know about that, Mr. Poirot. We have already had the funeral, and the burial is scheduled for tomorrow," said Jack Cavendish, Alexander's son, looking wary.

"I understand, but if we can determine the cause of death, then we may be able to find some closure and prevent any more tragedy in the future," said Poirot, his voice compassionate.

The family looked at each other, considering Poirot's words. Finally, Arabella spoke up. "You make a good point, Mr. Poirot. It would be best to know what really happened to Alexander . I will allow the autopsy to be performed."

"Thank you, I will arrange for the procedure immediately," said Poirot, rising to his feet. "Please accept my deepest sympathies once again. You have my word that I will do everything in my power to uncover the truth."

Poirot kept his word and arranged for the autopsy to be carried out. The results were surprising. Alexander Cavendish had died from a burst brain aneurysm, which was entirely natural and not suspicious at all.

It all began to make sense. Alexander Cavendish had been under immense pressure from Barton, who had been blackmailing him for months. Cavendish finally relented and changed his will, hoping to pacify Barton. However, the guilt of betraying his family and the stress he was under eventual caused his death.

Chapter 9:

After gathering the necessary evidence, Hercule Poirot, Captain Hastings, and Miss Marple proceeded to the local police station to present their findings. They were welcomed by the Chief Inspector who was curious about what they had discovered.

Poirot handed him a folder full of information, including the hotel staff's statements, George Barton's personal information, and the evidence he had gathered during his investigation. The Chief inspector was immediately absorbed in the documents, reading every page, finding a look of disbelief crossing his face.

"Mr. Barton seemed to be blackmailing Mr. Cavendish," Poirot explained calmly. "This was the reason he left the hotel without paying his bill, Mr. Cavendish was to pay."

Hastings added, "Furthermore, Barton had forced Mr. Cavendish to alter his will in his favour, which ultimately led to his death."

Miss Marple spoke up, "Mr. Cavendish was under a lot of stress due to the blackmail and had a collapse that led to his unfortunate death."

The Chief Inspector blinked twice before finally looking at them and saying, "That's a serious accusation, and we will need to investigate it thoroughly. I want you to accompany my colleagues back to the hotel and take us through everything that you have discovered."

Poirot, Hastings, and Miss Marple agreed to the Inspector's request and followed the police officers back to the hotel. The place was now bustling with police activity, with hotel staff and guests milling around the lobby nervously.

Poirot led the police through the case details and presented the evidence they'd collected, which left no doubt of Barton's guilt.

Chapter 10;

Poirot took the Chief Inspector aside and said "I have credible information that George Barton, is likely to attempt an escape through either the local railway or bus station. This lead has brought me to believe that George Barton's movements can be tracked by a thorough surveillance of these stations".

The Chief Inspector said "I have already alerted my team of officers to patrol the area outside and inside the railway and bus station. They have been equipped with walkie-talkies and a detailed description of the suspect. I have also requested that they look out for any suspicious behavior and report back to me immediately.

I have emphasized to my officers the need for constant vigilance, particularly during the peak hour rushes. It is possible that Barton may attempt to blend in with the crowd, so the presence of officers at all entry and exit points is crucial.

The railway and bus stations are obvious and convenient options for Barton because they provide several escape routes and multiple destinations to choose from, making it hard to predict where he may flee to. For this reason, I have expanded the search radius beyond the immediate vicinity of the stations, deploying additional personnel to check the adjoining area's.

Chapter 11:

George Barton stood on the platform of the small, quiet railway station, his eyes nervously scanning the surroundings. Barton was a wanted man, having been accused of blackmailing the late Mr. Cavendish for a hefty share in his will. He was trying to make his escape by catching the next train to London, where he hoped to start a new life and escape prosecution.

Barton had taken a calculated risk by boarding the train without proper funds, hoping to avoid being caught by the police. He had hoped that they wouldn't notice as he slipped through a back berth door and hoped he could evade them, but he wasn't so lucky.

Poirot was one step ahead of him yet again, and he stood on the platform, glaring at Barton as he tried to escape. Captain Hastings and Miss Marple were standing beside Poirot, and they could see the fear and panic rising in Barton's eyes as he realized that he was cornered and could not escape.

"George Barton, you're under arrest," Poirot announced in a firm voice, pulling out his identification card. "We have evidence that shows beyond doubt that you were responsible for the unfortunate death of Mr. Cavendish."

Barton tried to resist but was outnumbered by the police and the three detectives. He then gave up his attempts to run, murmuring a weak plea, "I was just trying to make a living. I never meant for anyone to get hurt," he admitted, his head slumping down to accept the inevitable.

The police handcuffed him and led him to a waiting police car, and Barton was taken into custody for questioning.

Chapter 12:

As a train whistle blew behind them, Hastings let out a sigh of relief, congratulating Poirot on another successful case. Miss Marple smiled, looking forward to enjoying a well-earned vacation, happy to assist in bringing about justice.

The trio embraced for a moment, their collective relief palpable, knowing that their determination and persistence had brought an end to Barton's sinister plans and corruption. For them, justice had been served.

Poirot smiled, feeling a sense of victory for having solved such a perplexing case. "The truth always comes out in the end, mon ami,"

Back home Poirot, Hastings and Miss Marple celebrated their victory with a bottle of champagne. They had done it again – solved a mystery that no one else could. However, it had been a tough case and it was only their persistence and determination that had led to the discovery of the truth.

As they toasted their success, Poirot turned to Miss Marple. "Merci, mon amie, for your assistance. Without your help, solving this case would not have been possible."

Miss Marple smiled, "It was my pleasure, mon cher. Anything to help solve a good mystery."

And with that, they all settled down to enjoy a well-earned glass of champagne, ready for the next mystery that would come along.

THE END